CEN' 1

MARRIAGE
MADE OF SECRETS

MARRIAGE MADE OF SECRETS

BY

MAYA BLAKE

First published in Great Britain 2013
by Mills & Boon, an imprint of Harlequin (UK) Limited,
Large Print edition 2014
Eton House, 18-24 Paradise Road,
Richmond, Surrey, TW9 1SR

© 2013 Maya Blake

ISBN: 978 0 263 24018 4

Harlequin (UK) Limited's policy is to use papers that
are natural, renewable and recyclable products and made
from wood grown in sustainable forests. The logging
and manufacturing processes conform to the legal
environmental regulations of the country of origin.

Printed and bound in Great Britain
by CPI Antony Rowe, Chippenham, Wiltshire

CHAPTER ONE

'*SIGNORA?*'

The voice, hesitant but insistent, jerked Ava from deep sleep. Momentarily disoriented, she pushed a swathe of Titian hair off her forehead but the nightmare…*that nightmare*…clung to the edges of her consciousness.

'I'm sorry to disturb you but *Signore* di Goia is on the phone. Again.' The stewardess, dressed in the emerald silk suit that displayed her employer's unique insignia, held out the sleek black phone. Ava eyed the phone, the same one she'd been presented with three times since the di Goia jet took off from Bali almost eight hours ago.

Different emotions replaced her irritation, dispersing the last of her dream-fuelled anxiety. The lingering sense of loss, which dogged her whenever she thought of Cesare, rose to mingle with the almost helpless excitement that thoughts of him elicited…

For a few seconds she forgot the heart-rending

devastation she'd left behind. Her mind crowded with the forceful presence of the man at the end of the phone. A man who despite being thousands of miles away, had the power to make her breath catch. The man who she knew within the depths of her soul she was losing with every second that passed.

'Please tell him, again, that I'll speak to him when we land.' She needed to conserve every ounce of her strength for what lay ahead.

The stewardess looked bewildered. 'But…he insists.' No doubt she'd never encountered another living being who refused to fall at Cesare di Goia's feet. Especially when that being was currently ensconced in unspeakably sumptuous luxury that barely began to epitomise the mind-boggling scale of the di Goia experience.

All around her, from the deep burgundy leather club chairs, the shiny cream marble tables to the bespoke silk-trimmed cashmere throws that graced every seat on the jet that could easily have carried several dozen passengers, Cesare di Goia's wealth and influence made itself forcefully blatant.

'*Signora?*' the anxious stewardess pressed.

Guilt for her predicament made Ava reach for the phone.

'Cesare.' She held her breath.

'Now you deign to answer my calls,' came the deep, tight voice.

'Why should I take your call when you've been avoiding mine for over two weeks now? You told me you'd return to Bali last week.' The ease with which he'd put her off made her hand tighten on the phone. It was with much the same afterthought that he'd conducted their marriage for the last year.

'I was delayed in Abu Dhabi. Unavoidably,' he added tautly.

Unavoidably. How many times had she heard that before? 'Of course. Was that all?'

An exhalation of ire came down the line. 'No, that is *not* all. Explain yourself,' came the unyielding command.

'I take it you mean: why have I commandeered your plane?'

'*Sì.* This was not the plan.'

'I know, but my plans have changed too. *Unavoidably,*' she replied with a lightness she didn't feel.

'In what way have your plans changed?' he bit out.

'If you'd bothered to pick up the phone in the last two weeks, I would've told you.'

'We have spoken in the last two weeks—'

'No, Cesare, you called twice, both times to

tell me you were postponing your return…' Her voice threatened to break as memories flooded her mind—her endless phone calls to Cesare's assistant to make sure his calendar was kept clear, shopping for the most enticing outfits and making sure the chef at the luxury rented villa in Bali prepared his favourite foods. She'd planned everything to the last detail…all in an effort to save her marriage. Only to have it backfire spectacularly. 'Anyway, I'm saving you the trouble of making the long trip, or of coming up with another excuse. Goodbye, Cesare.'

'Ava—'

She pressed the end button, cutting off the growled warning. She'd barely exhaled when the phone rang again. Carefully, she set it down on the table, unanswered.

The stunned look on the stewardess's face made Ava smile, despite the rush of her thundering pulse. 'Don't worry, his bark is worse than his bite.'

The woman coughed out an incoherent sound before hastily retreating to her station at the front of the plane.

With not quite steady hands, Ava poured a glass of water from the crystal-cut jug and took a tiny sip. Yes, Cesare ruled his world with unquestionable domination. But she'd never been one to ask *how high?* when told to jump, a fact which had, in the past, both intrigued and infuriated Cesare.

The past…before everything had settled into a passive indifference, before Cesare had slowly withdrawn from her, and chosen to stay in Rome more and more instead of at their home in Lake Como. Before the devastation of the South Pacific earthquake had shattered the last of her dreams of salvaging her family.

The decision she'd made so bravely in Bali yesterday now caused a thread of anxiety to weave inside her. Despite her bravado, her legs shook as she pushed aside her throw and padded down the long cream-carpeted aisle of the plane towards the smaller of the two bedrooms.

She turned the door handle.

Annabelle lay fast asleep. Soft light from elegant lamps illuminated her daughter's raven hair and long limbs splayed on the bed.

Unable to resist, Ava raised the camera slung around her neck and took a few quick shots, grateful for the near-silent clicks of the digital device.

Retreating just as silently, Ava returned to her seat, desperately trying to calm the hordes of steel butterflies trying to beat their way out of her. The last thing she wanted was to return home an emotional wreck. Her grip tightened on the camera.

The past month had been tormenting enough but she needed to be stronger still. She would need to be to stop hiding and face the truth.

Marry in haste...

Her insides twisted in pain and anxiety. Their coming together had been fast and furious. Right from the beginning, things had careened out of control. She'd been swept away by a passion she'd been unable to stem or understand.

But even in that maelstrom of whirlwind dates and mind-bending sex, Cesare had *felt* like the home she craved, the very essence of the family she'd never really had.

For a time...

This insanity needs to end! Cesare's heated confession when he'd taken her without mercy one day in a closet during a benefit dinner slammed through her mind.

Ironically, she'd found out she was pregnant with Annabelle the very next day.

And Cesare had begun to withdraw from her.

Shaking her head, she slid up the window screen, let a sliver of morning light warm her cheek, wishing it would also thaw her through. But it was no use. Inside, she felt cold, hard pain.

No. She couldn't—*wouldn't*—let him do this to her. If for no other reason, Annabelle deserved a parent who wasn't bogged down with acrimony. She deserved a mother who was content, at the very least. The family she'd craved and thought she'd found with Cesare had been a mirage. The sexy, powerfully dynamic man she'd married had changed into a man as coldly indifferent to her as her father had been.

And in her desperate desire to hold onto the illusion of what she'd probably never had, she'd nearly lost her daughter.

Annabelle had been through enough and Ava had no intention of letting her daughter suffer any more rejection.

'What the hell do you think you're playing at?'

Cesare di Goia's deep, dark-as-sin voice had the power to arrest her in her tracks; as did his impressive, hard-packed six feet two frame. Dressed in a pristine white open-necked polo shirt and black designer jeans that hugged lean hips and disgustingly powerful thighs, he stood tall and proud like any of the hundreds of statues that graced his homeland's capital city.

His black hair, damp from a recent shower, sprang from his forehead, looking even thicker and longer than when she'd last seen him. And he still said exactly what he thought when he felt like it and to hell with whoever heard him.

Damn him.

'Frighten the living daylights out of my child, why don't you?' Ava invited with soft sarcasm, while trying to calm Annabelle's sleepy squirming.

Eyes the colour of burnished gold shifted to Annabelle and a small grimace crossed his face. 'She's asleep,' he stated.

'Not for long if you keep growling like that. She's been through enough, Cesare. I won't have her upset.'

Tension radiated off his darkly tanned skin, so palpable she fought not to withdraw from it. 'Don't speak as if she's a stranger to me, Ava. I know exactly what she's been through.' His tone was framed almost conversationally but, although his voice had lowered, the fury in his deep tawny eyes had escalated in direct proportion.

'Forgive me for having to remind you, only you seem to have forgotten. Just as you seem to have forgotten *us.* Annabelle's emotions are still fragile, so dial back the hulk-smash attitude if you please. As to what I'm playing at, I thought I'd made myself perfectly clear.'

'Do you mean that highly informative one-line text that read: *We will arrive at 2pm* you sent seconds before my plane took off from Bali or the equally cryptic *my plans have changed too?*' he accused, making no move to shift his imposing frame from the doorway.

'Both.'

'Ava…' His voice was pure warning.

'Seriously, are you going to move or do you intend to carry on this conversation on the doorstep? What are you doing here, anyway? You hardly come to the villa any more.' Another sign of Cesare's withdrawal she'd ignored for far too long. She stared into his eyes, ignoring the warning that glinted in his narrowed gaze.

'What I'm doing here doesn't matter. You were supposed to wait in Bali until Annabelle was given the all-clear. Then I would've come for you.'

'The doctor gave Annabelle the all-clear three days ago.'

Surprise lit his eyes, then he looked beyond her shoulder to the car, his gaze searching. 'And Rita?'

'She was having nightmares of the earthquake. Once she was discharged from hospital, I booked her a flight home to London. She's racked with guilt—she thinks she failed Annabelle because she let go of her when the tremors started…' Recalling the nanny's inconsolable distress, a lance of pain—one of many that seemed ever ready to cause damage—went through her. 'I thought it was easier this way.'

Despite his grim look, Cesare nodded. 'I'll make sure she receives the proper treatment and severance package. But *you* didn't have to make this journey yet—'

'No, Cesare. Rita wasn't the only one who needed the comfort of home. *You* were supposed to return to Bali two weeks ago, only you were in *Singapore,* then in *New York.*'

He shoved a hand through his hair. 'This isn't really a good time for us to be doing this.'

'There hasn't been a good time for a very long time, Cesare.' A wave of sadness threatened to drown her but she straightened her spine and stood tall.

Tendrils of hair clung to her neck. Against her bare shoulders, the late afternoon sun singed her skin. If she didn't get out of the northern Italian sun, she'd be as red as a lobster by morning. 'We're home now. You should thank me for saving you the trouble. Now, are you going to deal with it or has being under one roof with us become a problem for you?'

His nostrils flared and his gaze dropped to Annabelle. 'It isn't a problem.'

Ava's grip tightened around her precious bundle. 'That's a relief. I'd hate for you to be *incon-venienced.*'

With Annabelle getting heavier by the second, the weariness of trying to keep a nearly-four-year-old entertained on a twelve-hour plane journey dug bone-deep. But she struggled not to show any weakness as Cesare continued to glare at her, his impressive body blocking the massive oak door-way to the Villa di Goia.

'Ava, we should've discussed this properly—'

'It's a good thing I'm not paranoid, Cesare, or I'd think you were trying to avoid me more than usual,' she snapped. When he didn't refute the al-legation, a shaft of ice pierced her heart. 'I think you're right, maybe this isn't the time to do this. I'll take Annabelle to my studio for a few hours. Let me know when you leave and we'll come home.'

She'd barely moved a step when a hand closed over her arm and jerked her back. She landed against hard, lean muscle. The scent that filled her nostrils was pure Cesare. A mixture of sandal-wood aftershave and man, it attacked her senses with the force of a spinning hurricane.

'No. Annabelle stays here with me.' Tension shimmered from the body plastered against hers.

'If you think I'm letting her out of my sight after

what she's been through, you're seriously deluded.'
She tried to pull away. He held on.

Heat spiralled upward, surging through her blood
like wildfire. The sensation, familiar yet unex-
pected, made her stumble. Cesare's hand tightened,
one hand coming to rest gently on Annabelle's
back as he steadied them both.

Pulse hammering, she glanced up. Dark emotion flashed through his eyes, quickly smothered
but nevertheless sparking along her every nerve
ending. The breath she sucked in felt as dry as
the desert. Fresh tingles shot down her spine and
she forced a swallow to ease the restriction in her
throat as he continued to hold her prisoner.

'I'll give you ten minutes to tell me of these new
plans of yours, then—'

'No, this is how it's going to work. First, I put
Annabelle down for her nap. Then we can have a
civilised conversation.'

He gave a low, deadly chuckle. *'Civilised?'* His
warm breath brushed her ear, sending heat-filled
tremors coursing through her body. 'Remember
how we met, *cara*?'

Sensation drenched her. Instantly she was
wrenched back to their first explosive meeting.

He'd almost run her down at a pedestrian crossing because she'd been distracted by the stunning

architecture of a centuries-old building she'd been trying to capture on her camera. The combination of near-death experience and the impact of his stunning looks had made her slam her fists down hard on the sun-baked bonnet of his blood-red Maserati.

His fury as he'd stepped out of his car to examine the damage had swiftly morphed into something even more dangerous, forbiddingly thrilling. 'We barely exchanged names before we were tearing each other's clothes off. *Dio mio,* you lost your virginity to me on the bonnet of my car within hours of us meeting!'

Memory's flames burned from head to toe. 'Is there a point to this?' she rasped.

'I'm just reminding you that nothing of our time together could ever be described as civilised, so let's not hang that particular label on it.'

'Speak for yourself. You might wish to wallow in caveman-like behaviour but I don't have to stoop to your level.' Somehow, she *would* overcome the riotous emotions Cesare engendered in her. For her daughter's sake.

Again, she pulled away. This time he let her go.

'Throw a gloss over it if you wish, *cara*. We both know the truth. When we let it free, our passion is uncontrollable.'

Eyes tracking her like a pitiless bird of prey eyeing a juicy rabbit, he pushed the door open, stood to one side and folded his arms.

For a second she couldn't move as she was drawn to the play of muscles underneath his shirt. Was it her imagination or were the hairs that peeked through his unbuttoned polo shirt even silkier?

Forcing her gaze away, she crossed the threshold of Lake Como's most breathtaking palazzo, the place she'd called home for the past four years.

The terracotta exterior with its multi-fountained courtyard, tiered gardens and baking paving stones sharply contrasted with the cool cream interior. High, perfectly preserved stuccoed walls framed vaulted ceilings where discreetly placed conditioners circulated cool air through the rooms.

On either side of the exquisitely trellised archways that fed the hallways leading to the four wings of the villa, tall shuttered windows had been thrown wide open, drenching the room with dazzling light.

A quick glance around was all she allowed herself but it was enough to make her catch her breath all over again. From the exquisite pieces arranged in the hallway to the impressive Renaissance art and family portraits that hung on the walls, the palazzo was still reminiscent of the time when the Villa di Goia had been a renowned museum. The Venetian marble and parquet floors beneath her feet gleamed with the opulent gloss only the super rich could afford.

'Nothing has changed since you were last here, Ava. I suggest you spend less time admiring the architecture and more time on explaining yourself. You now have eight minutes.' Tension seethed beneath the veneer of calm he presented.

She breathed in a deep breath and faced him. 'I suggest *you* stop the clock watching and help me with Annabelle. Unless you want a cranky child on your hands?'

The faint widening of his eyes was barely distinguishable, but she saw it nonetheless. Had the situation not been fraught with tension, Ava would've laughed. As it was, her daughter's weight seemed to be doubling by the second.

His lips firmed, then he stepped forward and calmly relieved her of her burden.

Ava heard a faint intake of breath as he hitched her close to his chest.

'She looks well,' he rasped, his voice a shade deeper.

'She is. The doctor is happy with her progress,' she stressed, flexing her arm to relieve the painful stinging needles.

More emotion flashed across Cesare's face as he continued to gaze at his daughter. Ava didn't need a crystal ball to divine that he was thinking of the last time he'd held her like this. The indescribable emotions that had gripped them both when they'd finally found her after the earthquake…

He turned abruptly towards the majestic sweep of stairs that led to the upper floors. His long strides made short work of the grand trellised staircase and she had to move quickly to keep up with him.

When he turned towards the east wing, Ava couldn't hide her surprise. 'You've relocated her bedroom?' Annabelle's room had previously been in the west wing.

'*Sì,* I've rearranged a few things. I wanted her to be close to me when she returned.' His voice was gruff, irritated, as if he didn't wish to be questioned. Another dagger of ice pierced her heart. *Me,* not *us.*

Following him into the room, Ava bit back a gasp.

The room had been redecorated in Annabelle's favourite colours of pink and green, complete with canopied bed. Toys of every description a child could want dotted the room but she noticed that the long-maned horses which were Annabelle's favourite were especially plentiful.

She watched as he gently placed Annabelle on the wide bed and stepped back. He waved her away when she stepped forward to help, and took off Annabelle's shoes and socks.

Pulling a light sheet over her shoulders, he plucked a stuffed horse off a shelf and laid it in the crook of her arm.

Pain scythed through her. How many times had she wished Cesare would do this when Annabelle was a baby? How many times had she dreamed of him bending down to kiss his daughter's forehead, murmur *buono notte, bambina*…?

She managed the pain for a second before he turned from the bed, his gaze slamming into hers.

'Come. Our daughter's presence is no longer an issue. Let's have that talk, shall we?' With purposeful strides, he headed for the door.

Tension emanated from the broad, set shoulders and, with every click of her heels on the marble floor, her own tension grew. She rubbed sweaty palms on the folds of her long skirt and suppressed the anxiety growing inside her.

She arrived in the living room to find him facing the large floor-to-ceiling windows overlooking the lush, perfectly manicured gardens and private mooring that abutted the world-famous lake. The view was so breathtaking, her fingers briefly itched for her camera before she forced herself to focus.

Cesare's gaze tracked a sleek speedboat skimming across the turquoise water but she knew his mind was locked in the room.

'You should've waited in Bali until I came to collect you, Ava.' He spoke without turning.

'I've never been good at taking orders without question, you know that. And you didn't seem to be in a particular hurry to bring us back home.'

'You had everything you needed.'

'Yes, the staff you hired for us were highly trained and extremely resourceful. I only had to lift a finger for my every wish to be catered for.'

'But?'

'But I'd had enough of being surrounded by complete strangers. It wasn't good for Annabelle. So here we are,' she said calmly.

'You should've told me!'

'What exactly is the problem here? Are you angry that I wanted to come home or annoyed that I dared to question your authority?'

He inhaled sharply. 'A lot has changed—'

'I'm very much aware of that. Staying away wasn't going to make it any better.'

'So why return earlier than we planned?' he enquired.

'Because this isn't just about you, Cesare. Life goes on and I need to make sure Annabelle returns to normal as quickly as possible. Besides, when I told you my plans had changed, I meant it. I've been contracted to cover the Marinello wedding.'

He frowned. 'You're an award-winning documentary photographer. When did you branch into covering celebrity weddings?'

'Annabelle needs to be around the familiar for the foreseeable future. I'm not taking her on assignment to the far reaches of the planet. She needs me to be here.'

His jaw tightened. 'The Marinello wedding is turning into a media circus. I won't have Annabelle exposed to that sort of environment.'

'I've never let my work disrupt her life in any way. It definitely won't this time round.'

'You didn't think to inform me of this Marinello thing before now?'

'Just take it as the side effect of my aversion to being abandoned.'

'You weren't abandoned. Annabelle needed medical care and she couldn't travel before then.'

'Yes, but that stay wasn't indefinite. Although I'm beginning to suspect maybe that's what you had in mind.'

'It wasn't. I agree that Annabelle needs to be home, but not…' He paused.

The cold grip on her spine intensified. 'Not your wife?' When he refused to reply, she let out a shaky breath. 'You don't have to say it, Cesare.' Her smile cracked around the edges. 'Annabelle's welfare is my priority right now. As long as she remains okay, you can go back to being indifferent to me. Or go back to Rome.'

A dangerous gleam flashed through his eyes. He balled his fists, his nostrils flaring. For a very long time he didn't speak. The air crackled with each charged heartbeat. Finally, he rasped, 'I'm staying here for the summer.'

Her heart skipped a beat, then immediately fell when she read the displeasure on his face. 'Then this is going to be *very* awkward for one of us.'

'I don't want you here. Not right now.'

The blunt words stung deep.

'Why not?'

'I'm in the middle of…' He stopped and shoved a hand through his hair. 'We both know things haven't been right between us for a while. But I can't be…distracted by anything right now.'

She pulled in a shaky breath and reminded herself why she was doing this. She set her bag down on the coffee table in the middle of the room.

'The state of your marriage is an inconvenient distraction?'

A nerve pulsed in his jaw. 'Especially the state of our marriage. If you'd stayed in Bali—'

'I didn't. You like to control people and things around you but I'm not one of them. This is your home as much as it is mine so I can't exactly throw you out. So you'll just have to tolerate my presence here, just like you have to tolerate your daughter.'

'Tolerate her? I'm her *father*.'

'Trust me, I know a thing or two about being *tolerated*. I don't think you'd want your performance as a father or husband to be rated. You wouldn't like the results.'

His colour receded a little beneath his vibrant tan and the room seemed to darken with turbulent forces. She watched him visibly swallow. 'If you want the civilised conversation you claim to want, I'd advise you to tread carefully, Ava. What is happening between us will *not* affect our daughter.'

She tried to stop the pain from biting deep. Selecting a seat as far away from his forceful presence as possible, she sat down.

'That's one thing we can agree on, at least. I suggest we set up a schedule. You spend time with her in the mornings while I meet with my clients; I'll take over in the afternoons. As long as she's happy, I need not interfere in…whatever it is you think I'm interrupting.'

He gave a harsh laugh. 'You're as non-interfering as a bull in a china shop.'

'Only when I need to be.' Like when confronted with an icily cold, angry, astoundingly gorgeous Italian male who threw out commands like they were sweets at a kids' party. Or when you grew up isolated in a house ruled by a distant father who treated you as if you were invisible and brothers who were more than happy to emulate their father. 'Sometimes it's the only way people take notice of you.'

'Is that why you've returned so suddenly? You want me to take notice of you?' he enquired with disquieting softness.

That voice, *that* precise, perfectly pitched cadence, bathed her skin in goose bumps that had nothing to do with pain and everything to do with unwanted memories. It threatened to dominate her senses. Forcing them away took much more effort than she was happy with. 'I'm here because my daughter needs to be home.'

Another dangerous gleam darkened his eyes. '*Our* daughter. She's as much mine as she is yours, Ava.'

She stormed to her feet. 'Really? You've barely

seen her in the past year. You choose to stay in Rome and make one excuse after another as to why you don't come home any more. So what are you doing here, really? What's changed? What's prompted this sudden yearning to play *papà?*'

A peculiar look crossed his face, too quick for her to assess its meaning. 'She's my daughter. My blood. There was never any question that I'd resume my parental rights.'

'*Resume!* You can't press *pause* on parenting every time you feel like it. So what, now you've suddenly found time to slot her into your schedule? For how long? What if another deal suddenly crops up in Abu Dhabi or Doha or Outer Mongolia? You'll press *pause* again and fly off in pursuit of your next venture?'

A frown darkened his brow. 'You think I'll abandon Annabelle for a business deal?'

'Oh, don't act so annoyed. How many times did you leave me to jet off to parts unknown when another too-good-to-miss deal cropped up?'

He waved her away like a troublesome fly. 'That was different.'

The uncaring delivery of his words stole her breath. 'You expect me to think things will change because we're talking about your daughter now instead of your wife? When you didn't have any trouble choosing business over returning to bring her from Bali?'

Ava had spent far too much time torturing herself with the *whys.* What she needed was to concern herself less with the *why?* and more with the *why now?* Cesare never made a move without calculating at least a dozen steps ahead. Which made his sudden decision to summer at Lake Como and demand to have his daughter all the more suspect.

Dangerously suspect.

'Things have changed, Ava.'

'Enlighten me, then. How *exactly* have things changed?'

His gaze slid away. 'The earthquake was an eye-opener for us all, I won't deny it. I agree that Annabelle needs the safe and familiar around her right now. Both our jobs are very demanding. If something unavoidable comes up, she'll be adequately cared for. Lucia will step in for now until I can hire another nanny. Between them, she'll be cared for around the clock.'

She sucked in a breath. 'Lord, you have the nerve to say the earthquake was an eye-opener but in the next breath you admit you'd happily abandon your daughter when the lure of a business deal proves too much!'

His stare turned icier. 'I'll make time for her as

much as possible, but my work doesn't stop just because it's the summer vacation. I can't just abandon it.'

'Of course you can't. I'm not even sure why I'm surprised. Cesare di Goia, venture capitalist with the Midas touch, hasn't changed one iota, has he—?'

'Annabelle turns four in a few weeks.'

Thrown by the sudden turn of the conversation, she frowned. 'Yes, I'm very much aware of that. I've made plans.'

He glanced at his sleek silver watch. 'But if you're covering the Marinello wedding, you'll need to be in Tuscany for the next three weeks.'

'I see you're well informed.'

He shrugged. 'For some reason, Agata Marinello seems to think I need updating on every detail of her son's wedding arrangements.'

'You're the guest of honour and your company is bankrolling Reynaldo Marinello's reality show. You don't need a crystal ball to suss why she wants to stay on your sweet side. Besides, I think all the guests receive email and social media updates.'

'Which is exactly why I've blocked her messages as of this morning.' A look of impatience crossed his face. 'I haven't even officially accepted the wedding invitation yet. Not with everything that's going on—' He stopped and shook his head. 'I'll ask for the jet to be refuelled. Paolo will deliver you to the airport within the hour to take you to Tuscany. Annabelle will remain here with me. When you're done with the wedding, we'll talk.' He started to cross the room towards the house intercom.

Feigning ease she didn't feel, she settled back in her chair and took her time to cross her legs. 'I see you're all about minimising your carbon footprint.'

He paused mid-stride. 'You know my line of work necessitates the use of a private jet. If I didn't, I'd suffer permanently from jet lag.'

'Yes, I'm sure all the environmental charities would love that explanation.' She'd aimed for spiky snark intended to win her further ground. Instead her reply faltered as her treacherous mind conjured up the very effective means by which Cesare conquered jetlag—the enormous king-size bed in the larger, chrome and grey bedroom of his Gulfstream. The silky satin sheets, the soft, decadent pillows…the en suite made-for-two shower…her intensely erotic initiation into the mile-high club…

She tried to stare him down, but heat slowly crawled up her neck, stung her cheeks. She knew her pale skin had given her away when a small *knowing* smile whispered over his lips.

'I'm sure they'll allow me this small concession given my support of their other eco-saving efforts. Now, if you've finished berating me, I'll instruct Lucia to provide you with some refreshments before you leave.' He walked towards the villa's intercom next to the extensive drinks cabinet and lifted the receiver.

Any lingering arousal fled as his statement sank in.

'The Marinellos changed their wedding venue three days ago—the official stance is a termite infestation at their Tuscany villa but I'm guessing *your* being here has something to do with the wedding's relocation to Lake Como.' She shrugged at his frown. 'I'm meeting with them tomorrow afternoon to discuss staging and the pre-wedding catalogue. But even that notwithstanding, I don't think you've quite grasped what I'm trying to tell you. Annabelle and I are a package deal, Cesare. Where I go, she goes.'

Slowly—excruciatingly slowly—he replaced the handset. Ava's heart thumped so hard against her ribs she feared the organ would expire from overuse.

'I warn you against rocking the boat, Ava. This isn't really the time to bring things to a head between us.' His voice was soft but edged in steel.

'And maybe you need to give up this false pretence of trying to play *papà,* return to Rome and just let us be.'

He lounged against the wall, sliding long fingers into his pockets in a display of utter calm. But she wasn't fooled. The lazy way his gaze raked her from head to toe only served to raise her hackles, along with her pulse rate.

Warning shrieked in her head. Cesare was most dangerous at his calmest. He hadn't built a globally successful venture capitalist company without being extremely calculating and ruthless where he needed to be.

He shrugged amiably, as if they were discussing which entrée to have. 'No, you're right. On second thoughts, maybe this is just what we need.'

A thread of trepidation unfurled in the pit of her stomach. 'And what exactly is *this?*'

'To have this marriage brought under the scrutiny it deserves,' he delivered. 'For us to stop avoiding the fact that this marriage is anything but a sham. Maybe once we face facts, I can get round to discussing the more important issue of custody of my daughter.'

Her laughter was so strained it scraped her throat. 'And you think when that happens I'd allow you anywhere near Annabelle?' It didn't click that she'd surged to her feet, that she'd bridged the gap between them, until her forefinger jabbed his chest. 'You really think any judge on earth would grant custody to a less than part-time father who's abandoned his daughter for most of her life?'

CHAPTER TWO

CESARE FLINCHED, THE sting of her words like whips lacerating his skin; the stab of her finger pierced like a knife in his chest. Raw pain pounded with every heartbeat as Ava's words barrelled into him.

He'd abandoned her.

When his daughter had needed him most, he'd failed her. He'd been unable to protect Annabelle...

Dark torment crept in, threatening to drown him every time he thought of what he'd let happen. He'd been too quick to believe...too swift to embrace his destiny.

And in choosing that path, he'd done the unforgivable.

The heart he thought had withered to nothing clenched hard. But within that torment, within the potent swirl of guilt and recrimination, a different emotion crept in.

Excitement. The guilt and recrimination were ever present, but alongside it a flood of hot excitement stole over his senses, awakening that treacherous desire he thought he'd slain a long time ago.

With every ounce of control he possessed, he tried to push it away, but like a drowning victim accepting the inevitable, he let it close in on him, submerge him deeper in its relentless maelstrom.

Dio, he felt…alive; from her single touch, he felt more alive than he had in a very long time. More than he deserved to feel after what he'd done.

Ava's finger jabbed him again, but all he could think, could feel, was how much cleaner the air smelled—richer, bringing a clarity that had eluded him for a long time.

'From the moment she was born, you abandoned her.' Her rough, pain-racked whisper stabbed deeper than if she'd shouted. 'And the day of the earthquake, you were supposed to spend time with her; instead you were on a *conference call!* You palmed her off on Rita—'

He wrenched back control and sucked in a breath. 'The minute I knew what was happening, I went in search of her. We both did. We tore apart that Bali marketplace with our bare hands.' Until they'd bled both inside and out.

Her hand dropped and she shook her head. 'Do you know how it feels to know neither of us were with her when the earthquake hit?' she whispered in anguish.

The thought tortured him day and night. '*Sì,* I know. I've lived with that horror every day since. I know how very easily we could've lost her. But I also thank God she was found.' *Someone else* had dug his daughter out of the submerged marketplace. *Someone else* had cared for Annabelle, taken her to the hospital and taken the time to put her photograph on the missing person's wall. 'We may not have found her ourselves but she was found,' he repeated. 'She was all right. She was *alive.*' Somehow, *miraculously,* his daughter had survived the devastating earthquake that had killed tens of thousands.

And, for as long as he lived, he intended to make sure his daughter never came to harm again.

'She was all right,' she repeated numbly. 'So you just thought you'd carry on being emotionally unavailable to her again?' Her words were hushed, but the pain behind them ripped through the silence.

Icy calm slowly built inside him, pushing aside his pain. Cesare welcomed it. 'I was there, Ava.'

Her face hardened and she folded her arms around her ribcage. 'You mean just like you're here now? In the same room but wishing you were somewhere else?'

His jaw tightened. Ava would never know how difficult it had been to keep from roaring his gut-ripping pain when he'd believed Annabelle was lost to him. She thought him cold. But he'd had to be, he'd had to shut off his emotions, to shut off any hint of yearning for what he couldn't have.

Except for Annabelle.

His daughter was the one thing he wasn't prepared to give up.

It'd taken him years to finally heed the warning he'd blindly ignored. To accept that he had no business taking a wife, never mind fathering a child.

He might be astute when it came to business but his personal relationships had always come at a price. A very steep price, he'd come to realise.

'And now you've decided you want your daughter you think you can just click your fingers to make it happen?'

'It was always going to happen. I'm sorry if you believed otherwise.' The horrendous events of the past few weeks had painfully brought home to him that Annabelle was the only child he'd ever have. And now she was here—albeit earlier than he'd anticipated—he had no intention of letting her go.

'Your arrogance is astounding, you know that?'

'Isn't it one of the things about me that turns you on?' He had the fleeting satisfaction of watching colour surge under her skin. Anger soon replaced her blush.

'Dream on. Your attraction level has dropped lower than the temperatures in the Antarctic.'

His fiery *moglie* had the tendency to lash out first and think about the consequences later. Wasn't that what had drawn him to her in the first place? Her vibrancy? Her blind, uncontrollable passion for life?

He sidestepped that reminder.

With a swish of her brightly coloured skirt, she stalked to the window. Cesare caught himself following the sway of her hips and reined himself in. Things were fast getting out of hand.

Again.

Their first meeting had been a heady, mind-blowing experience. She'd been a potion to end all sweet potions, lighting up his days, blazing through his nights like a spectacular comet. Against his every instinct, he'd let his guard down.

Once again he'd let a woman get under his skin. Something he'd sworn to himself and to his brother, Roberto, he'd never let happen again.

Cesare had walked out of his last meeting in Abu Dhabi the minute he'd learned Ava had summoned his plane. He'd even contemplated ordering his pilot to return her to Bali. But he'd known she would've found another way of achieving her goal.

She turned, arms folded in battle stance. He suppressed a grim smile. His Ava hadn't changed. Corner her and the fierce lioness emerged.

Except she wasn't his. He never should've taken her in the first place—although the exhilaration of being her first lover still made his blood pump faster—never should've placed the di Goia emerald on her finger…

His gaze fell to her bare fingers. 'Where is your wedding ring?' The burning need to know erased every other thought from his head.

Surprise widened eyes the same colour as the famous di Goia family heirloom. 'My wedding ring?' she echoed.

'*Sì.* Where is it?'

'In a box…somewhere. What does it matter?' she challenged.

Cesare had the completely irrational urge to grab her arms and shake her, demand to know why the ring wasn't on her finger. Instead, he jammed his fists into his pockets and forced himself to stay put.

'Just checking that you hadn't donated it to the commune you were growing fond of in Bali.'

Her arms tightened. 'I'm glad to see you think so highly of me, Cesare. And I don't need to pawn your jewellery off to help the causes I believe in. I'm more than well compensated for my job to fund my charitable endeavours.'

Did she realise how gripping her arms so tightly pushed her breasts up, so they looked even fuller, more tempting? The faint outline of her areolas against the white of her cotton halter top and the faint freckles marching across her chest sent the pulse kicking in his groin.

'Do you have a lover?'

Dio, where the hell had that come from? He raked unsteady fingers through his hair, the sheer astonishment his question caused clearly reflected in the slack-jawed look on Ava's face. But then was it really that astonishing? They'd spent so much time apart in the past year, he didn't even know which circle of friends she moved in these days.

Whose fault is that?

Her hand fluttered to her neck, crept around to her nape and flipped her flaming hair over one shoulder. He followed the movement, his fascination with the ripple of sunlight through the long tresses causing him to tense further.

'Don't you dare go there with me, Cesare,' she snapped.

Her non-answer made jealousy sear his insides. He'd distanced himself from her. She should be free to take other lovers. So why did his gut clench in sharp rejection of the idea?

'Why? Did the commune make you sign an oath of secrecy?'

'It wasn't a commune. And the people there are—'

'Eat, pray, love advocates?'

'No, believe it or not, they're professionals who've given up their time to help better the lives of others, especially the victims of the earthquake.'

'In the hope of *finding* themselves in the process?'

Her lips firmed. 'We can't all find ourselves in the next multi-billion euro deal, Cesare. Why did you abandon your daughter?'

He gripped his nape, renewed tension clawing through him. 'I thought it was better that I stay away. If it makes you feel better, call it an error of judgement on my part and leave it be.'

The understatement of the millennia. Marriage to Ava, *Dio,* to any woman, had never been on the cards for him. Not after what he'd put Roberto through. Not after Valentina...

In some ways, while he regretted the devastation it had wrought on countless lives, the earthquake had been his wake up call. His head had been wrenched violently from the sand. And now he had the rest of his life to made amends to his daughter.

'An error of judgement?' Ava shot back immediately, like a damned terrier intent on ravaging its favourite toy. 'Does that include our marriage?' she demanded.

Ignoring her, he strode to the drinks cabinet, curbing the urge to pour something stiff and bracing. He'd drunk himself into a stupor more than once this past year. He couldn't afford to do so now. He needed to stay focused on the female who prowled restlessly behind him.

'Answer me, Cesare. This…whatever's going on between us…is it another woman?' she persisted in that damned husky tone.

Bitter laughter escaped before he could stop it. He poured a tall glass of water and handed it to her. 'Why do women always think it's another woman?'

She gazed straight at him. 'Because men are as predictable as the tide during a full moon.'

'Would it make it easier if I said it was another woman?'

He didn't miss the shaft of pain that flitted through her eyes. Her lips wobbled before she pursed them. But her gaze didn't waver from his. '*Is* it?'

In a way he wished it had been as easy as infidelity. Because infidelity would mean he'd stop caring. Or wanting what he couldn't have.

'Turn down the Marinello gig. Return to your commune in Bali. Or take another assignment abroad. Give me the summer with Annabelle. We'll talk when you return.'

Her eyes flashed rebellious fire at him. 'No. Annabelle needs me. Besides, too much has happened for me to just up and leave on an assignment. I think deep down you know that.'

He silently conceded the point. The earthquake had changed things between Ava and him just as much as it'd altered his relationship towards his daughter. As much as he didn't want to admit it, looking at Ava in battle mode he hadn't witnessed for a long time, he knew in that instant he was screwed.

He gritted his teeth. 'The foreign minister is a close friend. You didn't become an Italian citizen when we married. All it would take is a single phone call and I can have you thrown out of the country. Do you realise that?' He threw out the straw-clutching Hail Mary.

'Yes,' she stated simply, not in the least bit cowed. 'But if I leave I take Annabelle with me.'

Against his will, his eyes strayed to the soft curve of her mouth. It would be as soft and supple as he remembered. Along with the rest of her.

Having her close would drive him crazy.

But the need to have his daughter close—to begin to repair the damage he'd caused outweighed all else. His internal debate lasted milliseconds.

'Fine. We'll both stay here for the summer.'

Her mouth dropped open, then her eyes narrowed. 'That was a little *too* easy.'

'Don't delude yourself, Ava. This isn't going to be easy for either of us. I know what you want and I can assure you I am unable to give it to you. What I can do is ensure Annabelle isn't caught in the crossfire of our...situation. You understand?'

She sucked in a ragged breath and Cesare knew he'd got through to her. The late afternoon sun slanting through the windows danced over her fiery hair as she nodded.

Grimly satisfied that his control was under firm guard, he headed for the door, ruthlessly suppressing the old sensations pulling at him, reminding him that his attraction to Ava had always held a fatalistic edge that had excited him.

Doomed him. He'd let it get out of hand the same

way he'd let the situation with Roberto and Valentina unravel…

'So, does that mean you agree to a truce? That you won't try anything *double-crossy* somewhere down the line?'

He turned back from the door.

Her eyes reflected a defiance that reluctantly sparked his admiration. None of his family or subordinates would dare press home their advantage this way.

But a line needed to be drawn. 'That very much depends on you, *cara*. Your innate inability to not rush in where angels fear to tread could prove your undoing.'

Her lips tightened. 'Are you calling me a fool?'

'I'm inviting you to prove me wrong. Stay out of my way for the next six weeks and I'll have no need to declare war on you.'

Ava frowned at the closed door, her mind a whirlpool of jumbled thoughts.

She walked over to the French windows and gazed at the sparkling infinity pool. Something was wrong with the picture Cesare was presenting her with.

Even as a newly-wed, she'd realised very quickly that business came first with Cesare. She'd lost count of the times he'd upped and left on a business trip on the strength of a single phone call.

Now, all of a sudden, he'd taken weeks off to spend his summer here.

She wanted to believe that living through a devastating earthquake had changed him…but it was painfully obvious that Cesare was determined to keep her at arm's length.

Although his attitude towards Annabelle had changed…

Recalling his face when he'd laid their daughter down for her nap, a bittersweet emotion filled her.

If Cesare meant to spend time with Annabelle, Ava welcomed that, although she couldn't stop the tiniest well of jealousy from rising up.

Pushing the doors open, she stepped onto the terrace. The palazzo baked in the late afternoon sun. Perfumed scents of lemon trees and the specially reared roses the team of gardeners took immense pride in mingled in the air. She inhaled deeply, letting the fragrance suffuse her senses. But the clarity she sought never materialised.

The holiday in Bali had been her last-ditch attempt to reconnect with Cesare. She'd failed spectacularly right from the get-go. That first week, he'd shut himself away in the luxury villa's study and worked until the early hours of each morning.

On the first morning of their second week, desperate for a break from the overwhelming evidence of her failure, she'd left the villa armed with her camera. She'd been taking pictures of the beautiful local wildlife when the earthquake struck.

Her insides clenched anew at the heart-rending three days they'd searched for Annabelle and Rita.

She shuddered and blinked back the rush of tears. Ironically, she'd felt closer to Cesare in those bleak moments they'd spent ripping apart the marketplace where Rita had been strolling with Annabelle than she'd felt in a long time.

Well, Cesare had been right about one thing… she was a fool.

The staff had unpacked and folded away her clothes in the master suite on the other side of Annabelle's room by the time she went upstairs. It took moments to confirm Cesare's *I've rearranged a few things* didn't mean he'd moved back into the suite they once shared but rather the one on the other side of Annabelle's room.

Ava refused to acknowledge the knot in the pit of her stomach and undressed. The sheer gold-coloured muslin curtains that framed the queen-sized bed had been caught up with white velvet rope.

Approaching the bed, she picked up her coffee-coloured kimono-style silk gown and went into the bathroom. Bypassing the sunken marble bath, she entered the shower cubicle. After a refreshing shower, she donned an ankle-length green and white flower-patterned skirt and white top and checked on Annabelle. Finding her still comfortably asleep, Ava slipped her feet into a pair of white thongs, grabbed her laptop and went downstairs.

The aim had been to head to the *salone* that hugged the western side of the villa and overlooked the stunning gardens. She'd always found that room soothing. But in the hallway she slowed, lingered, unable to stem the flood of memories from washing over her.

Her first time to the Villa di Goia had been on her honeymoon. Two weeks of bliss when they'd only come out of the bedroom to swim in the pool or for Cesare to teach her to waterski on the lake.

He'd wanted to take her somewhere exotic, but for a girl brought up in a dysfunctional working class home, who'd never travelled beyond the shores of England, Lake Como at the end of a hot summer had been exotic enough. And after being carried over the threshold and falling as swiftly and deeply in love with the charming elegance of the Villa di Goia as she had with its owner, she'd had no wish to be anywhere else.

Besotted fool that she'd been.

With an irritated shake of her head, she banished her thoughts. Through the window she caught another glimpse of the sparkling swimming pool and smiled at the thought of Annabelle's delight when her water-loving child was reunited with her favourite pool.

'If that's a smile of victory, I'd caution against being too precipitate,' a deep drawl sounded from behind her.

Cesare lounged against a Louis XVI credenza that had been in his family for four generations. Above him a portrait of another di Goia, long dead but no less imposing, stared down at her with similar unnerving tawny eyes. How long had the living di Goia stood there, silently watching her take the stupid trip down memory lane?

'Poor Cesare. I can see my being home fills you with all sorts of unhappy feelings. I get it. But I'm not going into hiding just to please you and I'm certainly not going to stop smiling in case it offends you.'

His smile mocked her. 'I have no problem with you smiling, *cara,* I just don't want you deluding yourself that you've won an easy victory.'

'I wouldn't dare. But remember your rule goes both ways. I can't stay out of your way if you insist on straying into mine.'

He straightened and sauntered towards her. 'Is this where we indulge in the childish game of who was here first?' he asked.

She shrugged. 'It's not childish. *I* was here first. And, if you must know, I was smiling at the thought of Annabelle being safely home and being surrounded by familiar things.' Ava caught herself, realising she didn't owe Cesare any explanation. 'Anyway, I'll let you reclaim your domain—'

'You weren't just thinking about our daughter. You were reminiscing about *us*.' He said it so calmly, so matter-of-factly, Ava felt a shiver race up her spine.

'You're wrong.' The need for denial was visceral.

'Liar. We may have been apart more than together for most of the past year, Ava, but you're still as easy to read as an open book.'

'Then it's a book whose language you don't quite fully understand. Because, from where I'm standing, you couldn't have got things more wrong if you'd tried.'

His jaw clenched, the mocking smile wiped clean. Part of Ava wanted to punch the air in triumph. The other just wanted to weep because if

she'd been as open as Cesare claimed, then it meant
he'd recognised her heart's one desire—the need
for the comfort of the loving family she'd never
had—and he'd still denied her.

'And, just so we're clear, my memories are my
own. They're not a subject for your amusement or
dissection.'

'Then learn to hide them better.'

'Why—do they make you uncomfortable? Would
you rather I strip myself of every humanising emotion, like you?' she challenged and immediately
bit her tongue when he tensed. The light pouring
through the tall shuttered windows carved his face
in taut, almost statue-like relief.

'You think I'm without emotion, *cara*?' he que-
ried so softly the hairs on her arms rose in desperate foreboding.

'Not where I'm concerned. When it comes to me,
you're as emotional as a plank of wood.'

His eyes narrowed. Almost in slow motion, she
watched his hands leave his pockets, reach up and
curl around her arms. One slid down, relieved her
of her laptop and set it carelessly aside.

'What are you doing?' Her question squeaked
out as he captured her nape.

He didn't answer, at least not verbally. The slow
burn in his eyes and the steady pressure of his fin-

gers on her skin told its own story. With effortless ease, he pulled her close. Ava actually heard her thonged feet screech across the floor in protest as he dragged her into stinging contact with his body. When he had her close enough, he boldly cupped her bottom.

'*Cesare!*'

Electric heat, wicked and powerful, snapped through her, zapping awake her senses with a force so potent she gasped. She should've wanted to move away from it. *Should've* worked harder to release herself from the powerful, chaotic destruction.

Instead, she found herself straining up to meet the havoc-causing mouth descending towards hers, pressing herself up against the heat of the rock-hard body.

His mouth slanted over hers, barely stopping to explore before his tongue slid through the parted welcome of her lips.

Somewhere in the outer regions of her mind, she knew she should feel shame for letting him kiss her thoroughly with so little resistance. But the pleasure racing unfettered through her was too heady, too blissful, to deny.

But she tried anyway. 'No…'

'Yes, most definitely, yes.' He tugged her closer.

With a soft moan, her hands settled on his chest. His polo shirt might as well have been non-existent as her hands stole over the hard contours of his muscled flesh.

When they slid around his neck, Cesare groaned. Heat erupted between them; the kiss grew fervent, rough. His tongue slid further inside her mouth, engaging hers in a rough play that made sweet fire rush to the apex of her thighs. Her nipples hardened into painful, rock-hard points. Boldly, she grabbed the hand at her nape and settled it over her breast.

He accepted her gift with a deep groan. One rough thumb grazed back and forth over her nipple, eliciting deep tremors of excitement within her.

If she'd thought distance and indifference would've lessened the power of Cesare's attraction, she was sadly mistaken. If anything, the deep chasm between them had only intensified her need.

She *yearned* for him with a hunger that deeply terrified her. Knowing she would joyfully have given anything she owned to feel his potent arousal deep inside her should've shocked her. Knowing she wanted nothing more than to sink to her knees, free his erection from the confines of his jeans and take him in her mouth the way he'd once loved her to, dismayed her. Yet, even as the thought struck, her hand was moving lower, seeking the silver square of his belt buckle.

When her hand brushed his erection, he jerked, then plunged his tongue deeper into her mouth. His fingers closed around her nipples, squeezed and teased repeatedly until she wanted to die with pleasure.

She grappled harder with the buckle. The more she tried, the more her fingers fumbled. Using both hands, she managed to pull the belt through one hoop. Just then Cesare slid one hand between her legs. She lost the use of her fingers as unrelenting pleasure ricocheted through her. Unerringly, he found her nub of need through her cotton panties. Her breathing grew ragged as she parted her legs to accommodate him.

His buckle forgotten, she grasped his arms to steady herself and drowned in bliss. Reality fogged. Had she just thrown her head back? Was that his tongue sliding over the highly sensitised skin on her neck, drawing her closer to the edge of her endurance?

'*Dio*, you're so hot!' he rasped.

'Only because you set me on fire.' Deep down, she knew that fire would be her undoing. But, for now, she remained blinded to everything but the storm raging within.

The sensation of being lifted registered, then the cool wall touched her back. Cesare increased the pressure of his fingers as his mouth captured one aching nipple. Mercilessly he teased, then his mouth returned to hers to smother her cries as she shuddered and fell headlong into cataclysmic ecstasy.

Slowly, sounds began to impinge as the force of her orgasm abated. Cesare's scent mingled with the smell of arousal coating the air. Another shudder raked her frame when he withdrew his fingers. As if he knew letting her go would cause her immediate collapse, he wedged one muscled leg firmly between her thighs.

Against her stomach, his arousal burned hot and heavy.

More sounds encroached. She stood, dishevelled, in the hallway of the villa, barely hidden behind a trellised arch. Any member of their household staff could walk past. But Ava didn't care. She'd just had a sizzling reminder of the potent lovemaking she'd experienced only with Cesare. Her senses had sprung to vivid life, her body readying itself for his fullest possession.

She looked into his face. Torrid heat blazed in

eyes that held the look of barely leashed hunger. Her gaze dropped to his lips. The force of her kiss had bruised his lips and the sight of it made her melt with wanting. She reached for his button. 'Your turn.'

Ava was woefully unprepared for the swiftness with which he clamped strong hands over hers. 'No.'

CHAPTER THREE

A SHARD OF ice splintered her post-orgasmic haze.

'You want me. I know you do,' she blurted, slightly dazed by the thought that he would deny what he felt. The evidence was unmistakable, even through the layers of their clothes.

He stepped away from her, but not far enough, as if he wanted to be close when she collapsed. And certainly her legs were unsteady enough to make that a distinct possibility.

'This wasn't about me.'

She looked into his eyes. Slowly his meaning sank in, obliterating her desperate, humiliating desire. 'You bastard.'

He took another step back. Suddenly the scent of their lovemaking—if she could call it that—nauseated her. Because it was the smell of her weakness.

'You wanted to humiliate me,' she said.

'I merely wanted to prove a point. Passion is an emotion, *cara*, one I relish in the right circumstances. But I *choose* not to let it rule my life.'

She lowered her eyes, chagrin eating like acid through her at how easily she'd fallen for his ploy. 'You mean I let it rule mine?' She wanted to slink away in shame, but she was damned if she'd give him the satisfaction.

'I've just demonstrated that this is so.'

'Wow, so that display was all for me? Well, I hope you're proud of yourself.'

He stepped closer and slowly passed a finger over her swollen lip. '*Sì,* I am. And it's good to know I can still reduce you to putty.' His tone reeked smugness.

She didn't rise to the bait. They both knew he'd won this round. She straightened her clothes. 'Sure, you can dominate me with the sheer force of your sexual prowess. The orgasm you gave me just now? Out of this world. I'm a red-blooded female after all. But you've also proved that you're so cold-hearted you can control your life to the point where nothing touches you unless you want it to. So pardon me if I don't wholeheartedly buy your reasons for being here.'

He let go of her as if she'd suddenly developed a contagious disease. For a moment he looked almost…disarmed. But she didn't feel victory, just an emptiness that grew larger with each passing second.

'You're trying to rile me.' The face of the man who regarded her wasn't the Cesare who'd kissed her senseless moments ago, whose heart she'd felt beating unsteadily against her own. This was Cesare back in control, the master in complete command of his world.

'I'm speaking the truth. Deal with it.'

'It seriously terrifies me how prone to recklessness you can be.' With cool poise, he reached down and picked up her laptop. 'If you want to maintain that truce, I think we need to establish some ground rules. Come.'

Without waiting for her agreement, he strode off in the direction of his study.

By the time she found enough strength to straighten away from the wall and follow, he'd disappeared.

She found him seated behind his massive antique desk, his fingers steepled against his mouth. If he'd been any other man, she would've suspected he was hiding behind the desk to avoid her. But Cesare was no ordinary man.

He'd just proven catastrophically and conclusively that he could turn her brainless with desire, ride through the storm of passion with her, and emerge unscathed.

'If you're going to dissect what just happened—'

'What happened just now doesn't need dissection,' he said, cutting across her. 'But I do want to discuss Annabelle and the impact our being together will have on her.'

She frowned. 'Why should it impact on her?'

He ignored her question. 'How did she take Rita leaving? I know they were close.' His gaze bored into her with the force of a laser drill.

'She was distressed, of course, but—'

'You also said she's a bit more sensitive than she used to be.'

Her hackles rose. 'And you think this is in some way my fault?'

He exhaled. 'I'm not laying blame, Ava. I'm just trying to find the best way to settle her without causing her any more upset.'

'She's back home where she belongs, and I'll be with her every day. A loving family is what she needs.'

Tawny eyes hardened a touch. 'You'll be working some of the time.' His gaze strayed to her laptop, which now sat on his desk. 'You cut back on your work when we got married. Why the sudden return to full-time work?'

'Because I found out that playing the role of neglected wife isn't all that challenging—I could do it with my eyes closed, in fact. I needed something more.'

'Is that supposed to be some sort of statement?' he asked.

'You're the genius. Work it out.'

'You're my wife, Ava, and therefore my responsibility—'

'Isn't that a mere technicality?' She ignored his icy glare. 'You can't have it both ways, Cesare. We've been drifting apart almost from the moment Annabelle was born. Hell, we've barely lived together for the last year. Calling me your wife when it suits you or as a means of salving your conscience—what there is of it—is disingenuous. Your career has always been your first priority so don't you dare question my dedication to mine. You can continue to provide for your daughter, but I can more than take care of myself financially.'

'Nice speech. Although I see you didn't hesitate to make use of my jet when you needed it. You can't have it both ways either, *cara*. While we live under the same roof you're my responsibility and we both do what's best for Annabelle. We share all meal times with our daughter. And at all times we present a united front.'

'To show her *Mummy* and *Papà* don't hate each other?' she threw at him.

His mocking smile displayed perfectly formed white teeth. 'Her Mummy and *Papà* don't hate each other. I think I proved that conclusively just now.'

A residual post-orgasmic shiver raked her insides at the reminder. 'Sexual desire without a solid foundation fizzles out eventually, Cesare.'

One dark eyebrow tilted upward. 'Is this another enlightened nugget you were fed in your commune or did you conduct a personal study?'

'I don't need a study to tell me that it won't be long before Annabelle starts asking probing questions. She's beginning to notice that her kindergarten friends have mummies and daddies who live together. Last month, before we left for Bali, she asked me why you don't live with us. Those are the easy questions, so prepare yourself for the tough questions because they're just around the corner.'

With the swiftness of a flash flood, the smile disappeared and a veil descended over his bronze features. Before her eyes, he withdrew behind a veneer of cool indifference. 'Many couples live apart. When the time is right, we will explain things to her.'

'I can't wait because I'd quite like some answers myself. For instance, why are you wearing your wedding ring again? You weren't last month.'

He glanced at the simple gold band on his finger, a peculiar look crossing his features. It dissipated so quickly she almost missed it. But its haunting quality lodged a stone in her chest.

Before she could question it, his desk phone rang. His gaze flicked over her as he reached for it. 'I've arranged for dinner to be served earlier tonight, at six-thirty, for Annabelle's sake. We'll decide then on the best routine for all of us going forward.'

For an insane second, she wanted to rip the phone out of his hands, chuck it through the window and demand he answer her questions. But he'd already swung his leather seat towards the window, shutting her out as if she'd ceased to exist for him.

She grabbed her laptop and marched from the room before the temptation to smash it over his head overcame her.

A headache niggled at her temples. Although tempted to blame it on the effects of travelling through several time zones, she knew Cesare was the reason for it.

From the start, he'd imprinted himself so indelibly on her psyche that it had seemed as if Fate herself had willed it so. Even now, she only had to see him to feel a part of her unravelling, for her insides to weaken.

She hated herself for those weak moments almost as much as she hated herself for what she'd let happen in the hallway. It'd only taken a handful of minutes for him to reduce her from a sane, rational woman to a heap of shuddering wantonness. And for him to gloat about it.

She entered the *salone*, walked past the sumptuous green and white overstuffed chairs and whitewashed tables and chose her favourite seat—an elegantly carved chaise longue facing the breathtaking view of the lake.

After switching on her laptop, she resolutely fished out her iPod and stuck the earphones on in the hope that the music would drown out the sinking realisation that she only had to think about Cesare for him to take a hold of her mind and, it seemed, her body.

Clicking on the application she needed, she read over the list of locations she needed to visit and typed up a suitable schedule and the cameras she would require.

Reynaldo Marinello and Tina Sanchez were the Posh and Becks of Italy. The renowned footballer's engagement to his pop-star girlfriend six months ago had sparked a media frenzy, which Ava normally tried to avoid.

Witnessing the post-earthquake devastation in Bali, however, had sparked a need to raise awareness and money for disaster-stricken areas through her photography—which meant she couldn't afford to turn down lucrative assignments like these.

The Marinello pre-wedding catalogue would entail photographing various members of the prestigious Marinello family around the Lake Como area, with special emphasis on the bride and groom. Mind-numbing work, but if it enabled her to stay close to Annabelle she didn't mind one little bit.

Almost an hour later, Ava removed her earphones as a maid entered with a tray that held a tall pitcher of homemade lemonade and pastries. On her heels, Cesare strode in, carrying a wide-awake Annabelle, who in turn clutched a bright red toy horse with flowing mane.

'Mummy, *Papà* woke me up,' her daughter said. 'I had a bad dream.'

Irrational guilt sparked as Cesare's cool gaze met hers.

'She tells me she has bad dreams sometimes. You didn't tell me about them,' he said almost conversationally, but she didn't miss the steely undertone.

'The doctor said it was to be expected, after her trauma.'

'Look, Mummy, I have a pretty horsey.' Annabelle's demand helped her tear her gaze from Cesare's accusatory stare.

'I can see that. It's gorgeous.' She tried to keep her voice light.

'*Papà* got it specially for me.' Her daughter's wary gaze darted to her father. At his smile, hers widened a touch.

'You're a lucky little girl,' said Ava. Her laptop trilled as it shut down.

Cesare's gaze zeroed in on it and she was mildly surprised the machine didn't incinerate under the laser beam of his disapproval.

Shoving it aside, she stood. Cesare's scent, coupled with the freshly washed smell from her daughter, caused an intense pang of pain to dart through her.

Hastily, she stepped back and busied herself with pouring drinks, refusing to let her mind flash back to the hallway incident. Annabelle gulped her drink down and immediately jumped down again, ready to reacquaint herself with her home.

'I asked if there was anything else I should know. You didn't think I needed to know about her nightmares?' he rasped fiercely.

Ava bit her lip. 'They started last week, after I sent Rita home. She calms down when she knows I'm nearby.'

Cesare swore fluently under his breath. 'I needed to know, Ava.'

She nodded. 'This was why I wanted to come back. She's always been happier here.'

His jaw clamped so tight a pulse kicked in his temple. 'You will tell me everything, no matter how small or insignificant. Agreed?'

The power behind his words rocked her to the core. From near total distance to this fierce protectiveness of Annabelle made her reel. That she had a destructive force of nature to thank tightened chaotic knots in her stomach. 'Agreed.'

After several seconds, he relaxed.

'So,' Cesare drawled, his gaze following Annabelle, who'd picked up Ava's iPod, inserted one earphone and was now dancing around the room, 'your commune didn't just teach you to eat, pray and love, did they also teach little girls how to dance like eccentric rock stars?'

Ava found herself taking her first easy breath since she'd arrived back home. 'Just because you can't dance to save your life doesn't mean you can look down your nose at others. Besides, she gets her dancing gene from me.'

'No doubt about that,' he drawled.

'Watch it!'

Annabelle danced over to them. 'Can I have a biscuit, please?'

Cesare picked up the plate and held it out to her. 'It's called *biscotti*. Try saying it, *piccolina*.' He smiled with undisguised pride when she pronounced it perfectly.

Ava swallowed but the solid lump wouldn't move from her throat. Blinking away sudden tears, she jumped up and picked up her laptop.

'If you don't mind watching her, I'll go and put this away.'

'Then we can swim, Mummy? You promised.' As a prize for being good on the plane, she'd promised her daughter the earth—and a long swim when they got home.

'Yes, we can, so don't have too much lemonade, okay?'

As she left the room, she felt Cesare's incisive gaze probing her back. Her steps quickened, defiantly trying to outrun the calm, completely rational voice asking if she knew what she was letting herself in for.

They weren't in the *salone* or at the pool when she returned five minutes later, dressed in an orange one-piece swimsuit and white shorts with a loose white shirt over the top. Ava was about to return indoors when she heard her daughter's voice.

Following the flower-lined pathway that curved round the villa, she stopped in her tracks. Cesare and Annabelle were bent over a rose bush, admiring a trio of butterflies fluttering from one bud to the other.

It wasn't the picture of wonderment on her daughter's face that stopped Ava's heart. It was the look of intense pain reflected in Cesare's face as he gazed at Annabelle. He looked so starkly distraught that she leaned her hand against the wall to steady herself.

And immediately pulled back with a gasp as the baking concrete singed her hand. Cesare glanced up. In an instant the look was gone. If it hadn't registered for more than a few seconds, Ava would've thought she'd imagined it. She held her breath as he straightened up and strode to her.

'Are you all right?' he questioned coolly.

'Hot wall, bare skin. Bad idea. Should remember that.'

He claimed her hand and examined the heated flesh. 'There's some ice on the table. I'll put some on it for you,' he said.

She glanced at Annabelle.

'She's enthralled with her butterflies for now.

Come.' The word was more command than suggestion.

'Seriously, it's nothing.'

He cast her a grim smile and marched her to the poolside. 'Is that why you're grimacing? Because it's nothing?'

'Fine, it hurts like hell. Satisfied?'

Pushing her into one of the padded seats, he sat opposite her. 'Why do women always say *it's nothing,* when clearly it isn't?'

'I don't know. You've probably known more women than me. You tell me.'

He didn't deny it. Just smiled in that oh-so-smug way that made her yearn to kick him. Hard. 'Normally, it's just a way of attracting more attention.'

Irritation grew, along with her already heated temperature. He'd used the fully equipped pool house to change into swimming trunks in the time she'd gone upstairs and his bare muscular thighs almost imprisoning hers were covered in short silky hairs that taunted her with their luxuriant promise. The reaction it caused to her body was as unwelcome as it was unstoppable.

'You think I burned myself deliberately to get your attention? You really think I'm that pathetic?' Why did her voice sound so husky? And why, when he hadn't even administered the ice on her stinging palm, were her nipples peaking so painfully?

He smiled, wrapped several ice cubes in a linen napkin and placed it in her palm. 'No, *cara mia*. Because you're not most women.' His gaze captured hers, the tawny depths smoky, intense and way too captivating for her sanity.

'Thank you. I think.' Foolish pleasure stole through her, accelerating her already racing heartbeat.

'Prego.' The deep, softly muttered word flowed over her overheating senses.

Everything fell away. The sound of the water splashing against the side of the pool, the warm buzzing of bees in the afternoon air, the sound of boats on the lake. Everything, except the heat radiating from Cesare's eyes, the warmth of the fingers curled around hers and the emotions rippling through her. His gaze traced her face. When it lingered on her lips, it took all her willpower not to lick them in shameless anticipation.

Unavoidably, her own gaze fell to the sensual curve of his lips; lips she'd tasted mere hours ago.

Heat collected and oozed between her legs, stinging with a need that gripped with relentless force. Realising she hadn't taken a breath in a dizzyingly long time, she sucked in air through her mouth.

The sound ripped through their sensual cocoon, intensifying the tension arcing between them. Cesare swallowed, the movement of his strong neck making her pulse skitter and her fingers yearn to caress his skin.

His fingers convulsed around hers. Her gaze returned to his face and found his attention riveted on her breasts.

Desire wove a dangerous path through her as she remembered how much he'd once loved her breasts. How he'd used to mould them, shape them with his hands and worship them for what seemed like long, endless hours while he murmured heated Italian words in homage.

His gaze darted back to hers and she knew he was remembering too. Remembering how he'd loved them even more when they grew fuller with her pregnancy.

She couldn't take it any more. Her eyelids grew heavy, her blood thickening with unbearable yearning even as she tried to pull away.

He held her easily.

'Cesare…' She wasn't sure whether she was pleading or protesting.

His eyes darkened to a burnished gold. He wanted her too. *Desperately*. The thought sent delight racing through her veins at the exact moment he gave a strangled groan.

'Cesare, please.' She wasn't even certain that she wanted him to answer the sexual need clawing through her. All she knew was that she wanted *answers.*

She saw his withdrawal even before Annabelle's distressed voice reached them. '*Papà,* they flew away. I wanted them to stay but the butterflies flew away!'

'*Mi dispiace, piccolina,* but these things happen. It wasn't meant to be.'

She knew his words were directed at her. He continued to stare at her as he curled her fingers over the napkin and placed her hand on the table.

She closed her eyes, willing away the intense pain spiralling through her. *Breathe…just breathe. In. Out.* Over the sound of her fracturing emotions, she heard Cesare soothe his daughter's disappointment.

What about me? What about this gaping ache I carry inside because I don't know what's happened to us?

Questions crowded in her head as she sat there, the ice doing its job to soothe her palm while, inside, confusion congealed into a tight ball behind her breastbone. Slowly it dawned on her that she'd let it happen again; she'd let Cesare toy with her emotions, disrupt her thought patterns until she wasn't sure whether she was coming or going.

Dear Lord, she'd been in his presence less than half a day and already she'd let him weave his potent spell around her twice. *What was wrong with her?*

Intensely irritated with herself, she let Cesare take over entertaining Annabelle, listening to her delight as he swam up and down the pool with her on his back.

Dinner was brought out to the poolside just as the sun started to sink over the lake. Annabelle started to flag soon after with the effects of jet lag. By the time Cesare carried her upstairs, she was almost asleep.

Weariness sapped Ava as she lingered over Annabelle's bedtime story. For a moment she contemplated walking through to her own suite, crawling under the covers and letting the whole world fall away.

No. She straightened her spine.

Cesare had demonstrated in the last year that he could erase her comprehensively from his life. That he had every intention of continuing to do so.

But, for the sake of her sanity, Ava needed to know *why.*

* * *

Cesare picked up his wine glass and tried to marshal his thoughts. But even *thinking* had become a gut-wrenchingly difficult task. Unbidden, the scent of Ava's orgasm rose to torture him. *Dio*, he'd been close—so close—to experiencing that sweet heaven again. But he knew, as much as it killed him, he had to walk way. And continue walking away. Every single time.

For Roberto's sake, as some small, pitiful measure of penance for what he'd done to his brother, he couldn't give in to the craving.

Besides, the last thing he needed on top of the trauma and devastation life had thrown his way was the complication sex brought. Especially the uncontrollable kind that always felt a heartbeat away whenever he touched Ava.

This afternoon he'd boldly laid down his plan for ensuring he and Ava wouldn't run into each other more than necessary for the next few weeks. But already he saw the plan unravelling. The incident in the hallway and the few hours he'd spent with her by the pool had refuelled the sizzling attraction he'd tried and failed to bury. An attraction he had no right to rekindle. Or crave.

That only left him with one option.

Light female footsteps approached. Cradling his

wine glass in one hand, he watched Ava emerge onto the terrace, child monitor in hand and a look of fierce determination in her eyes.

Although his heart sank a little, a part of him welcomed the situation.

Because, if nothing else, being caught in the middle of an earthquake had hammered home just how unpredictable life could be. He'd ruined his brother's life. He refused to remain in a situation where he could ruin another.

He'd tried to reason with Ava. Now it was time to be cruel to be kind.

She stopped in front of him and set down the monitor. 'I'm hoping being home will make them stop, but if she has another nightmare we'll hear her.'

He merely nodded. A flash caught and drew his attention to his wedding ring. He'd slipped it on when he'd lunched with his mother during his quick stopover in Rome. His parents had suffered enough in the last month; the last thing he'd wanted was to distress them further by exposing the state of his marriage.

Before him, Ava shifted from one foot to the other. Then she exhaled. 'What you said this afternoon…about things not meant to be. What did you mean?' she demanded, her arms once again crossed in battle stance.

He took his time to twirl his wine glass, allowed his gaze to rise slowly from her bare, stunning legs, linger at her rounded hips, past her deliciously full breasts, to capture hers.

His grim smile felt as strained as the tightening in his groin. 'When we met, I was blown away by your beauty. You were sexy, vivacious, with a reckless streak that drew me like a moth to a flame. And the sex…' His breath stalled, his pulse kicking up another dangerous notch. 'The sex was unbelievable, better or quite possibly the best I'd ever had.' Her shocked gasp bounced over him and disappeared in the night breeze. 'Unfortunately, I let it blind me into making an unforgivable error.'

Her eyes darkened. 'What was that error?' she whispered.

He threw back his drink in one greedy, hopefully fortifying gulp and set the glass down. 'I think you'll agree that catastrophe has a way of bringing into sharp focus what's important.'

'Yes.'

'Two things became clear to me in the aftermath of the earthquake, *cara mia*. The first was that my daughter means more to me than my life itself and I would rip my heart out before I let anything remotely close to that devastation happen to her again.'

The fire in her eyes told him she felt the same. For a moment, he didn't want to utter the next words, but he knew he needed to. 'The second was that I…as deliciously tempting as you were…as mind-altering as the sex was, *bellissima*, I know now that I should never have married you.'

CHAPTER FOUR

I SHOULD NEVER have married you.

Ava stabbed the trowel deeper into the soil, oblivious to the heat and sweat cascading down her face. A grim smile stretched her lips as she recalled the horror on Lucia's face when she'd asked for the gardening supplies.

But it had been that or go mad from replaying that statement in her head over and over. Agata Marinello's endless text messages every two seconds hadn't helped to improve her disposition either.

Hard physical labour was what she needed. Bone tiredness meant she would collapse exhausted into bed at night and fall asleep without torturing herself with thoughts she had no business thinking.

For the past week, Cesare had stuck religiously to the schedule they'd set out on her return. He spent time with Annabelle in the morning while she met with the Marinellos; she took over in the afternoons and they had supper with their daughter before they took turns giving her a bath and putting her to bed.

Living under the same roof as Cesare was going smoothly. The truce was working. She should've been happy.

She wasn't. A very unladylike snort escaped her throat. How could she be when she was constantly in knots over Cesare's behaviour? The man had proved himself a champion at avoiding her, yet she could feel his presence as closely as the air on her skin. Could sense his gaze on her from his window when she played at the pool with Annabelle or when they went down the jetty to watch the luxury boats sail by. What was frustrating her most was the longing she could sense in his gaze.

Cesare yearned to spend more time with his daughter, but he was keeping away because of her. Had she really got it so wrong? Had her need for a family blinded her to the fact that she was setting up that family with a man who didn't want the full package?

Pain ripped through her and her fingers stilled as she tried to recall for what seemed like the millionth time, when things had started to change.

Cesare had been shocked by her pregnancy, even though he bounced back almost immediately. Hell, she was sure he'd been ecstatic.

He'd been a godsend during her pregnancy. Unbelievably, the sex had been her favourite part of being pregnant—the seemingly innocent back rubs that had often reached very pleasurable conclusions.

A flush suffused her face in recollection of the times he'd only had to whisper *back rub* in her ear to make her pulse race.

Then Annabelle had been born. Cesare had taken one of his rare trips to visit Roberto. And then, seemingly overnight, everything had changed.

She slammed the trowel into the soil.

'Careful there, *cara*, or you'll petrify the seeds before they get a chance to grow.'

'Careful there, Cesare, or you'll lose a foot if you annoy me.' She silently cursed him for his ability to move so quietly despite his impressive size. If it'd been one of her brothers, she'd have had no compunction in biting his head off. In fact, she'd done so many times with Nathan, the youngest of her three brothers.

But her emotions were too raw, too close to the surface to risk losing control in front of Cesare. She took a deep breath.

'*Bene poi,* since I value my foot way too much, I'll stay out of harm's way.' Droll amusement tinged his voice and she gritted her teeth not to react to it.

'What do you want?' Her surly voice matched her mood.

'You mean aside from checking that my land isn't being desecrated by your vicious digging?' he asked.

She sat back on her heels and glared at him. 'You own more than your fair share of land in Italy and the western world. I'm sure you won't miss a six by ten foot square piece.'

He shrugged, disgustingly unperturbed by her censure. 'Lucia tells me you're growing oranges. You do remember we have oranges delivered fresh every day from my orchard in Tuscany, don't you?'

'These are miniature oranges,' she replied, trying not to let her eyes wander over the stunning perfection of his lean, hard-packed frame.

From her disadvantaged kneeling position, he seemed even more devastating, more domineering in a way that made her struggle to hide a small shiver of desire.

'Ah,' he retorted. 'So you prefer your oranges small?'

'The oranges aren't small, only the trees—' She stopped when she saw the mocking smile that flashed across his face.

He was making fun of her. Disconcertingly, she wanted to grin in response. She bit her lip hard to hide its Judas twitch.

'What do you want?'

He held out her phone. 'It's been pinging text messages every few minutes. I thought they might be important.'

She took it and flung it on to the grass. 'Agata Marinello and her unending demands can go to hell. Was that all?'

He didn't answer immediately. In fact he remained silent for so long that she glanced up at him.

The trace of a smile had vanished. His gaze was disturbingly intent as he stared down at her. Her throat dried as she experienced a sudden, inexplicable feeling that he was about to tell her something she wouldn't welcome.

'We have a guest coming to dinner this evening.' The notice was delivered with little warmth and no pleasure.

She frowned. 'You seem unhappy about it.'

His lips pursed. 'I'd prefer not to have any company but it is what it is.'

'Tell them not to come then,' she said simply. 'What would be worse, begging off hosting a dinner or exposing the guest to an unwelcome reception?'

'It would be discourteous of me since I myself arranged it a…while ago.'

Her heart lurched unsteadily as it occurred to her that Cesare's displeasure didn't stem from having an unwelcome guest, but from Ava's presence at the dinner table. 'You mean before I decided to bring myself and my daughter back home unannounced?'

'Something like that.'

She cleared a sudden painful constriction in her throat. 'Is it a business dinner?'

'No, Celine is a friend of the family and is…important to me.'

'Celine?' Why had her insides suddenly gone cold despite the sun's intense heat?

Cesare had invited a woman to dinner. Big deal. But she couldn't stop the sudden tension making her fingers tighten around the trowel. Dull pain shot up her arm. Even then she couldn't let go of the tool.

Cesare had friends. Not that she knew many of them. Theirs had been a jealously guarded courtship, preferred by both of them because she didn't have to share Cesare with her disapproving family and he'd been based in London at the time with easily ignored business acquaintances.

She'd met his parents at the wedding, although not his younger brother, Roberto. She'd also been introduced to the smattering of uncles, aunts and cousins that Italian families abounded with—a family she'd been desperate to become a part of. A family that had on face value welcomed her— until Cesare's gradual distance had quickly become a family-wide phenomenon.

Her memory wasn't faulty enough to have forgotten a *Celine*. And certainly not one who was *important* to Cesare.

'Ava?'

She realised she'd missed his question.

'Sorry—what?' The words were forced through stiff lips.

'I asked if seven-thirty was okay with you,' he repeated slowly, as if making allowances for her sluggish brain.

Was seven-thirty okay with her? 'No.' It slipped out before courtesy or caution could stop it.

'Perdono?'

'You asked if the time was okay, I said no. It's obvious you don't want her here now I'm back. Use me as the excuse. Tell her not to come because the time is not okay with me.'

This way, she'd never have to meet the *important* Celine, never have to endure her gut twisting in knots the way it was now at the prospect of meeting the woman who might one day replace her and wear the famous di Goia wedding ring Cesare had presented to her with such dignified pride the day he'd proposed to *her*.

Cesare's clear disbelief at her response almost made her laugh out loud. *Almost.*

'As much as I appreciate your *selfless* efforts, unfortunately it doesn't work that way.'

'Well, can I be excused? She is *your* guest, after all.' Why did she have to break bread with the woman?

Anger laced his movements as he shoved his hands in his pockets. 'You will be dressed appropriately and ready to greet our guest at seven-thirty, Ava. Do I make myself clear?'

'Ooh, I love it when you go all domineering and masterful,' she purred, only to gasp as he sank down to her level, bringing six feet two of bristling masculinity up close and very personal.

'Did the consequences of last week teach you nothing about challenging me?' he asked in a deceptively soft tone.

Ava knew she was playing with fire, but she couldn't seem to stop herself from testing the depths of the flames. 'You mean pushing us both to the edge before withdrawing? I don't know, you tell me. I'm still digesting your *I should never have married you.* How long does blue balls last?' she taunted.

'*Che diavolo*—' His jaw actually slackened before he managed to clench it tight again. When he spoke again, it was between gritted teeth. 'Just be ready at seven-thirty. *Capito?*'

'If I must.' She raised the trowel in a mock salute and watched him stalk away, shoulders stiff with tension.

With renewed vigour, she dug into the earth. In a few hours she would meet Cesare's *important* guest.

Maybe the gods would be kind and make Celine short, fat and dumpy as all hell.

The gods granted her one wish.

Celine *was* short.

But fat and dumpy she was not. She was the original pocket Venus, with the kind of fragility that made men want to instinctively take care of her, in a way that made Ava, with her five foot seven frame and the three-inch heels she'd slipped into as an added confidence booster, feel like the *Lean-*

ing Tower of Pisa as she reached out to shake Celine's proffered hand.

Celine di Montezuma reeked cute perfection from the top of her expensively styled gleaming black hair to the pointy toes of her designer heels. What grated the most were her open friendliness and genuine, pleasant smile she directed at Ava as she removed her silk wrap and handed it to Cesare.

'I've heard so much about you,' she said to Ava.

'Really? I hadn't heard so much as a peep about you until four hours ago.'

Ava ignored the warning glint in Cesare's eyes as he straightened from cheek-kissing Celine.

Their guest's warm laugh echoed in the vast hallway. 'He didn't just drop my visit on you, did he? Don't you hate that about men?'

'*Hate* is too mild a word.'

She laughed again and tucked her arm through Ava's. As much as Ava wanted to hate her, she grudgingly, painfully understood Cesare's attraction to the vivacious Celine.

The feeling increased all through Lucia's superbly prepared dinner of egg and salmon frittata starter, followed by slow-cooked lamb in herb sauce and diced potatoes. Which she hardly touched.

The lump that had lodged in her chest since Cesare announced her arrival grew with each second she watched the warm interplay between the two Italians.

For the first time since her return, Ava saw Cesare smile with genuine affection at another adult. The whites of his teeth gleamed in the subdued lights of the dining room as he responded to some joke Celine made.

Picking up her glass, she drained the last of the white wine she'd nursed throughout the meal.

Cesare slid her a narrow-eyed glance.

What? she wanted to blurt out. If he was callous enough to force her to watch him and his new paramour enjoy each other, then she could damn well get drunk doing it.

As if sensing the change in the air, Celine turned to her with a slightly wary look.

'How is Annabelle?' she asked.

Had Cesare tensed just then? Unfortunately Ava's head had started to swim from the sudden intake of alcohol and she couldn't be sure. Certainly, his fingers seemed to cup his wine glass a little tighter. Her gaze darted to his face, but his expression reflected arrogant calm.

Ava answered. 'She's fine, thank you for asking.'

'Is she adjusting well to being back home?'

'Sun, lake, swimming pool and all the toys a

little girl could have, thanks to a suddenly attentive and over-indulgent father. What's not to like?' She couldn't quite curb the sarcasm that emerged with her answer.

Celine's smile slipped another notch.

Watch it, Cesare's gaze warned.

Drop dead, she threw back. He shouldn't have invited her if he expected her to play nice with his girlfriend.

'I was hoping to see her this evening,' Celine said, breaking into the tense silence.

Surprise and more than a little anger surged through Ava, until she remembered she wasn't supposed to have been here when Cesare invited Celine to dinner.

Was that what he'd planned all along? Had he made plans to get rid of her and spend the summer with Annabelle and Celine?

The sheer scale of Cesare's anger at her arrival suddenly fell into place.

Pain swiftly replaced surprise. Calmly she placed her wine glass on the table. She didn't think the crystal was safe in her hand any more because the sudden urge to throw it at Cesare's head had gained astronomical proportions.

How dared he arrange for Annabelle to meet his girlfriend…without consulting her?

She shot him a glance. His cool, composed expression told her the same story it had since she'd got to know him. Cesare answered to no one. He did what he wanted when it suited him. And if he wanted to introduce his mistress to his daughter tonight, that was exactly what he would have done.

Except he hadn't. They'd put Annabelle to bed together with no mention of her meeting his guest.

'She's asleep. We put her to bed over an hour ago,' Ava responded since Cesare didn't seem inclined to.

'Oh.' Celine's disappointment made Ava experience a small fizz of gleeful satisfaction. 'Perhaps I can just look in on her?'

Glee and satisfaction evaporated. 'You want to look in on her?'

Again Cesare didn't seem surprised by the odd request. When Ava glanced at him, he merely shrugged and carried on twirling the stem of his glass between his fingers.

Ava swallowed down the heated *Over my dead body* that sprang to her lips. It was clear Celine was very much a fixture in Cesare's life. Whether it was tonight or another night in the very near future, Celine and her daughter would meet.

But it didn't have to be tonight, an irrational pain-filled voice whispered in her head. *It might happen, but it didn't have to be right now!*

'I don't think it's a good idea—'

Cesare pushed back his chair, and rising to his feet, halted her words. 'Come, Celine. I'll take you.'

'No you won't!'

His smile brushed the outer fringes of courtesy. 'Don't worry, Ava. She won't be disturbed. I'll make sure of it.'

He rose and beckoned Celine. The other woman's clear discomfort made Ava cringe inside but she forced her chin up and smiled despite the tide of acid anxiety that swallowed her whole.

'Make sure you don't. If she wakes up she'll be impossible to put back to sleep.'

Cesare didn't turn around as he escorted Celine out of the dining room, their footsteps echoing in tandem down the hallway.

Ava sat frozen in her seat, unable to stem the ever-increasing tidal wave of despair. A small part of her hadn't quite accepted it when Cesare told her Celine was important to him. Even through the ordeal of dinner, a small part of her had hoped that she was nothing more than a fond family friend.

But would a *family friend* insist on seeing Annabelle after being told she was asleep?

Of course not. Which meant, the woman whom her daughter might soon be calling stepmother was now upstairs, looking in on her precious daughter…

…while she sat here, clutching her figurative pearls like a tragic, overdramatic Victorian heroine.

Swift burning anger propelled her upright. She reached the sweeping staircase before she remembered she'd discarded her shoes under the dining table.

Whispered voices as she reached halfway up the marble stairs made her thankful for her bare, silent feet. Her hand curled over the smooth wood of the banister, her heart in her throat as she froze on the step.

'How long are you going to keep this from her?' Celine questioned passionately.

Cesare responded in Italian, his delivery too quick for Ava to follow, but she sensed it wasn't what the other woman had expected to hear.

Another burst of Italian, this time from Celine, resulted in Cesare's heavier footsteps heading towards the landing, and Ava.

'*No.* It's impossible,' he responded in an implacable voice.

Ava held her breath as they both came into view,

Celine's short steps quickening to catch up with Cesare's longer strides.

'It's painful, I know, but you have to tell her. She deserves to know what's going on.'

Cesare reached the stairs, saw her and froze. A second later, Celine spotted Ava too. Her eyes widened with alarm before they shut in dismay.

Cesare's mouth opened but no words emerged. His hands balled into fists and his piercing eyes bored into hers with a mixture of anger and frustration.

Ava tried to swallow, but the throat muscles required wouldn't comply. Her fingers tightened around the banister and she prayed desperately that her legs would support her for just a little while longer.

'Ava…' Cesare finally rasped.

But her pain was too sharp, too decimating for her to stand there, listening to whatever explanation his astute brain had swiftly concocted for her.

'Save it, Cesare. I may be slow on the uptake, but I'm not stupid.'

His colour faded considerably beneath his tan. A look, curiously close to alarm skittered over his face as he braced a hand on the post next to him.

'So…you know?'

The depth of his reaction to her discovery only

increased her despair. She glanced at Celine, who stood clutching the rail—as white as a sheet.

For a second Ava wondered whether she would go all out and add to the overly dramatic scene by performing a Victorian swoon, perhaps save herself the embarrassment of a confrontation by fainting. But Celine stayed on her feet, even though her hand managed to find Cesare's arm and grip it.

Tearing her gaze from that proprietorial display, she addressed Celine. 'I know you're sleeping with my husband, if that's what you're so anxious for him to tell me.'

Cesare sucked in a swift breath. '*Dio mio*—'

'But as long as we're still husband and wife, you'll stay away from him and from our daughter. Do you understand?'

Celine shook her head. 'No! *Per favore,* Ava—'

Ava raised her chin. 'It's *Signora* di Goia to you. Now, get out of my house.'

CHAPTER FIVE

'*MADRE DI DIO,* Ava, there are no half measures with you, are there? You always have to jump in with both feet.' Cesare had just slammed the door behind a hastily departed Celine. The fury radiating from his body made her swallow nervously.

She flipped her hair over her shoulder in a show of bravado that was fast fading in the face of his anger. 'If you mean I don't tolerate being made a fool of in my own home, then the answer is yes.'

'Need I remind you that we're all but separated and this is *my* house?'

She shrugged. 'What's yours is supposed to be mine too, isn't it? I'm sure I've seen that tattooed on a body part somewhere.'

'*Porca miseria.* You insult our guest and all you can do is crack jokes?'

'You should've warned me you were sleeping with her. Maybe then I would've been on my best behaviour!'

His eyes narrowed, his fury intensifying by the

second. 'I'm *not* sleeping with Celine,' he said through gritted teeth.

'Oh, don't take me for a fool. You two were making enough moon eyes at each other to keep this villa illuminated for a month!'

'I've known her for a very long time. There is a familiarity between us—'

'Yes, it's called *sex*.'

He took an unchecked step towards her, as if to physically restrain her from speaking. At the last moment he lurched away and stalked to the window. Shoving his fists into his pockets, he stared out into the softly lit garden.

'Celine is the daughter of one of my father's oldest friends. I've known her since she was born. We've always been friends but she was much closer to Roberto.'

Ava tensed at the mention of his brother's name.

For as long as they'd been married, Cesare had remained close-lipped about his reclusive younger brother. All she'd ever been able to find out was that he lived in a castle high up in the Swiss Alps and only permitted Cesare to visit him from time to time. Ava had never been told why Roberto di Goia had withdrawn from the world.

'So Celine is Roberto's friend, not your girlfriend?' Stupid hope flared to life.

He shrugged. 'I think our respective parents hoped Celine and Roberto would marry one day. I know Celine waited a long time for Roberto to propose.'

'You mean before he went to live in Switzerland?'

'Yes.' The word emerged with a poignancy that scraped her heart.

'Don't tell me. The proposal Celine wanted never arrived and now your parents want you to step in and do the right thing by her? Honour the agreement or something?'

He turned from the window, his tawny eyes gleaming with grim amusement in the half-light. 'You've watched too many vintage *mafioso* movies, Ava. No one *demands* honour marriages like those any more. There was never any agreement, just a wish.'

A pang of discomfort made her realise she was twisting her fingers into knots. 'So what happened between Roberto and Celine?'

The fleeting amusement faded, to be replaced by a pain so deep and gut-wrenching she took a step towards him. 'Cesare?'

He didn't respond for a long while, his bleak gaze fixed in the middle distance. Finally, he heaved a heavy sigh.

'I should've told you… I'm sorry, there didn't seem to be the right time to announce that sort of thing.'

She frowned. 'Announce what? What didn't you tell me?'

'Roberto…' He stopped and another pain-filled sigh ripped from his chest. Fear clutched Ava's chest.

She bit her tongue, torn between screaming for an answer and the need to protect him from the obvious pain of what he fought to say.

The need to know won out. 'What about Roberto?'

He inhaled again. 'He…died two weeks ago.'

Shock ripped through her. '*What*?'

Cesare shot her a dark, tormented look. Then he glanced absently around the room. When his gaze returned to hers, his features were once again resolute.

'Roberto is dead. Celine never got the chance to marry him. The fact that she didn't doesn't mean I see her as anything more than a friend, so you can contain your hysteria about us having an affair. And I would appreciate you curbing any such future outbursts in front of our guests.'

This was the Cesare she knew—commanding, resolute, domineering.

He strode past her, ready to walk out.

She grabbed his arm. 'Wait! You can't just announce that Roberto is…you can't just drop something like that and walk away. Why didn't you tell me this earlier?'

Another flash of pain crossed his eyes. 'Think about what's happened between us lately—the earthquake, the trauma you and Annabelle have been through. When do you suggest I should've dropped this on you?'

'You could've found a way to tell me. He was my brother-in-law—'

'A brother-in-law you never met.'

'And why was that? You've always been reluctant to talk about Roberto, what happened to him or why you two weren't close.'

His eyes grew bleaker. 'Leave it, Ava.'

'Why should I? You accuse me of jumping to the wrong conclusions. How can I arrive at the right one when I seem to be operating in the dark? Tell me what happened between you and Roberto.'

For a long time she thought he wouldn't answer. 'Valentina happened,' he slid out.

Ava was almost too afraid to ask. 'Who's Valentina?'

'Celine's older sister. Seven years ago, I'd just opened my New York office when I met her at a party. She was thinking of relocating and she had a good head for numbers so when she asked me for a job, I offered her one.'

'Did you sleep with her?' The words shot out before she could stop herself.

His eyelids descended. 'Ava…'

'It's okay; it was before we met. I guess I have no right to ask you that.' Although the jealousy that seared her insides told a very different story.

'The answer is no, I didn't sleep with her. But Roberto thought I had. He turned up in New York a month later and accused me of poaching his woman. Turns out they'd been dating in Rome before she came to New York. I didn't know.'

'Hell. Surely you explained things to Roberto?'

He gave a bitter laugh. 'Until I was blue in the face. But he wasn't in a listening mood. We had the mother of all fights, right in the middle of a meeting in full view of my board members.' He paced to the window and turned back sharply. 'Unfortunately, that wasn't the worst of it. In the middle of all that carnage, Valentina announced she was pregnant with Roberto's child.'

Ava frowned. 'How was that worse?'

'Roberto got down on one knee there and then and asked her to marry him. She declined his proposal.'

'Oh no.'

'I got the blame for that too but I convinced him not to give up so he kept trying. She told him she wasn't ready to get married or settle down, even though she intended to keep the baby. Roberto begged her to return to Rome with him. I think he wore her out in the end...'

'But...?'

'Roberto never truly believed the child was his—Valentina liked to party hard and often. He talked her into having an amniocentesis. She nearly lost the baby.'

Ava gasped. 'Oh my God.'

'After that she flatly refused to stay with Roberto. She came back to New York...asked for her job back. She was carrying my brother's child. I could hardly say no.'

'And Roberto blamed you all over again?'

He shrugged. 'We'd never been particularly close growing up. He was ill more often than not, constantly in and out of hospital as a child, while I was away at boarding school ten months out of twelve. Valentina was his first and only serious relationship.'

Her heart clenched hard. 'So the big brother he thought had everything had swooped in and stolen the only woman he cared about.'

Cesare's jaw clenched hard. '*Si*. He refused to believe that I'd had no hand in Valentina's defection. Nothing I said made a difference. I tried to talk to Valentina but she refused to return to Rome.' He sighed. 'I gave her all the support I could. In hindsight, I think I may have given her too much support.'

'She never went back to Roberto?' The question slid from numb lips as it struck her just how very little she really knew about the man she'd married.

'No, she never got the chance.' His husky reply broke through her thoughts. 'She overdosed on sleeping pills midway through her second trimester. Turned out she was manic-depressive and her state had been heightened by her pregnancy. Roberto lost his mind with grief. He cut me off, he cut our parents off and moved to Switzerland.'

Ice drenched her soul and, for the first time in her life, Ava found herself struck dumb. Neither of them moved for what seemed like an eternity.

Then he exhaled a harsh breath. 'You wanted to know. Now you know.'

The words hit her like a slap in the face. 'You still should've told me. At the very least our child deserved to know she'd lost her uncle.'

His gaze slid away. 'Roberto died two weeks

after the earthquake. I didn't think it was fair to burden you with that news.'

'And in the time since then? You could've texted, emailed…hell, you could've Tweeted me, for heaven's sake.'

A rough hand shoved through his hair. 'Yes, I could've done all of that. But I didn't. Let's just chalk it up to me being the heartless bastard you think I am and move on, shall we?'

Ava wanted to rail at him but, seeing the grief behind his words, she opted for peace. 'Will you at least tell Annabelle? She deserves to know.'

Cesare's gaze met hers and Ava's heart caught at the pain in the dark depths. '*Sì,* I'll tell her about Roberto when the time is right.'

A thought niggled, but danced away before Ava could fully grasp it. 'Was that what Celine meant when she insisted you tell me?'

'She thought you needed to know about Roberto, yes.' His tone implied he would very much prefer if she dropped the subject. Pain stung again.

The niggling persisted. 'But why did she insist on seeing Annabelle? It all seemed a bit OTT to me, to be honest.'

A grim smile crossed his mouth. 'Celine, like most women, doesn't know the meaning of subtle. She knows about the earthquake and has been asking to visit since you and Annabelle returned. She takes her role of honorary aunt very seriously.'

'As long as that's the only role she's banking on.'

'Drop it, Ava.' The warning was back in his voice, tension sizzling in that flattened line of his mouth. 'You insulted her and jumped to the wrong conclusions. You should thank your lucky stars I'm not rescinding our truce after that performance.'

Her heartbeat thundered. 'It's your fault. If you'd told me all of this *before* she arrived, we wouldn't be having this conversation!'

Cesare pinched the bridge of his nose. 'You push me…all the time you push. You never stop.'

The bone-deep weariness behind his words pulled her up short. 'What do you mean?'

Tawny eyes turned grave. 'From the very beginning you pinned high hopes on me—your need for a family, for *togetherness*. Don't think I didn't know what the Bali trip was all about. Did it occur to you that I wasn't in a position to provide you with all of that?'

Ice skated down her spine. 'Where is this coming from? If you felt like this, then why did you bother to come to Bali?'

He looked away. 'You rarely ask me for anything any more. You asked for that and I couldn't refuse you.'

'So you came anyway, knowing I was trying to save our marriage but knowing you had no intention of engaging with me?'

'I was hoping you'd see we were beyond help.'

'Well, silly me. That sailed right over my head.'

His jaw tightened. 'I was wrong, of course, to think things would go smoothly with you around; wrong to think I would be spared the reminder that I've failed you.'

'I'm just trying to understand—'

'Understand why I don't fit into your mould of a perfect husband and father? Because, above all else, it's what you want, isn't it?'

'*Above all else?* God, you make me sound like a needy, pathetic creature.' He remained silent and the ice unfurled. 'Is that what you really think of me?'

'I've never been good at the family thing, Ava. My parents had their hands full with Roberto. He was their number one priority for a very long time. Don't get me wrong, I wasn't neglected but I learned very quickly to be content with my own company. After a while, I preferred it.'

'Then why marry me?'

'You were carrying my child.'

The numbing ice encased her whole being. He stilled for a moment then jerked closer, the edges of regret on his face as he lifted his hand. She ducked out of reach before he could touch her.

'You don't need to soften the blow,' she forced out. 'In all things I would prefer brutal honesty.'

'Has it ever occurred to you that I keep you in the dark for your own protection?'

'I'm not a child, Cesare. And I especially don't want to be kept in the dark about things that affect our daughter. I want the truth. Always.'

A bleak look entered his eyes and his shoulders stiffened. 'In that case you need to know something else,' he said.

Her heart lurched. 'What?'

'Although he was sick on and off for months, we don't actually know what Roberto succumbed to in the end. That was part of the reason for Celine's visit.'

'Her…what *exactly* does Celine do?'

'She's a doctor.'

Her brain cogs slowly engaged until his meaning sank in. 'So asking about Annabelle…?'

'She also wanted to check on her *medically*. On all of us.'

Fear tightened her chest. 'What does she think could be wrong? And please don't sugar-coat the truth to protect me.'

'We honestly don't know. Roberto refused medical treatment in the weeks before his death. It could even be that he took his own life.' Raw pain drenched every word.

'*Suicide?*' she rasped. 'Dear God.' She sank into the chair. After several minutes, she raised her head. 'Is there anything else I should know?'

He visibly pulled in the reins of his control. 'No. The results of the cause of death should be available in the next few days. But tomorrow morning we'll call Celine and you'll apologise for your behaviour. *Si?*' The soft, dangerous tone sent sweet shudders chasing up her spine, melting the ice just a little.

'And if I refuse?'

'*Cristo,* why do you challenge me at every turn?'

'Because I'm not a doormat. You liked that about me once, remember?'

'I'm not in the mood to reminisce about us.'

She wanted to tear her gaze away, to stomp away in fury, but she was frozen, held captive by the magic of his voice, the seductive uniqueness of his scent that filled her senses, made her want to linger a while longer, breathing him in.

'If you meant what you just said about your… deficiencies, I think it's in all of our best interest that we tackle the subject of *us* sooner or later, don't you think?'

'Don't push me tonight, Ava. I'm at my limit.'

Something softened inside her. 'Not tonight.' She stepped closer, an invisible cord pulling her to him, his heat a craving she couldn't resist. Tentatively, she touched his firm cheek. 'I'm truly sorry about Roberto. Will you tell me if there's anything I can do?'

He muttered something low under his breath. Incoherent and pithy, but it caught and stopped her breath nevertheless. Mesmerised, she watched one hand come up slowly, building her anticipation as it touched and traced the skin underneath her ear.

She shuddered. The pad of one finger traced the vein pulsing heated, frantic blood through her body. Her breath grew shallow, causing her heart to accelerate even more from the lack of oxygen. When his finger came to rest on the pulse at her throat, it was all she could do not to moan.

He caught her to him, one strong arm snagging her waist and lifting her off her feet like a pirate claiming his bounty.

His mouth replaced his finger and she moaned at the relentless drum of desire beating in the swollen flesh between her legs, at the urgent tightening of her nipples. But he didn't relent. He lapped her flesh with his tongue, driving her nearly out of her mind before he sucked, deeply, mercilessly.

Oh dear God, she'd have a mark on there tomorrow, blatant evidence of Cesare's rough possession.

But right at that moment Ava didn't care about anything except prolonging the pleasure of Cesare's hot mouth on her. Eagerly, she tilted her head, offering the sensitive expanse of her neck to him.

With a groan he accepted her offer, kissing the length of her throat and back again, before biting hungrily on her soft lobe.

Her nails dug into his shoulders. Holding on tight, she lifted and threw her legs around his waist, anchoring herself against the pleasure of his lean frame. The hard rigid evidence of his arousal grazed her damp panties.

The shockingly intimate position made them both tense, then draw together as if unable to resist the magnetic force of the desire arcing between them.

When he started raining kisses along her jaw, she turned her head, met his mouth in a fierce kiss that rocked them both. She was hardly aware of him moving, barely aware of the firm sofa behind her back as he lowered her onto it.

All she knew and craved was Cesare, above her, around her. Everywhere but inside her, where she desperately needed him to be.

Frustration bit deep. Tightening her thigh muscles, she tried to draw him closer to the centre of her, to the place that wept for his possession.

'You do this to me every time,' he said against her lips. 'You drench me in this…this *insanity.*'

'You make me sound like some witch, wielding a potent spell.'

The moment the words left her lips she regretted them. Because, just like the first afternoon of her return, her voice reacted like ice on his skin.

Tense muscles locked in fierce rejection as he disentangled her from his body. Face taut, he levered himself away and stared down at her. When he stumbled backwards, she clutched his arm.

'Please tell me this wasn't another stupid caveman demonstration?'

His pupils dilated and she glimpsed his turmoil before, with jerky movements, he removed himself to the other side of the room.

'It wasn't an intentional one, no,' he replied huskily.

'Then what exactly was it? God, Cesare, you're blowing so hot and cold, anyone would think you were a virgin.'

His face tightened. 'You don't know what you're asking, Ava.'

And she had a feeling she would regret the

words, but her need to be with him, to experience the sheer bliss of Cesare's lovemaking had pushed her past shame. 'You're my husband. I'm your wife, albeit an unwanted one. What could be simpler?'

He whirled around. 'We haven't had sex in almost a year.'

A harsh laugh left her throat. 'Trust me, I *know*. And I'm not sure whether to be ashamed because I've let myself accept this preposterous situation between us or disgusted with myself because, despite everything, I still want you.'

His smile was tinged with an arrogance that made her palms itch to slap it off his face. Then kiss him like he was her last breath. 'Our chemistry defies reason and description. Always has. But you're chasing a dream, *cara*. One that can never become reality.'

She stopped and licked her lips. 'Then why are you still here?' Knowing he still wanted her, still desired her enough to shake his formidable control made her bolder.

Cesare had always prided himself on his control. It was only with her, on occasion, that she'd seen his formidable willpower slip. She'd suspected for a long time that he resented her for that loss of control.

She watched his hands unclench, and immediately clench again. 'Because it's becoming physically impossible to stay away from you.'

His gaze locked on hers, studying every movement like a predator tracking a doomed prey. 'Now it's your turn. You know I can't give you the wholesome family you want. What are you prepared to settle for?'

The white-hot gaze slid down to linger on her lips. She knew exactly what that look meant, and yes, she could have settled for wild, untamed, skin-melting sex. But she knew it would never make her happy. 'I'm not prepared to settle.'

Her heart thudded as he gathered himself together. His features hardened, closed off as completely as a solid steel door slamming in her face.

'Then we have nothing left to talk about.'

Pain rushed like an icy river through her veins. Gasping in air, she lowered her head to hide the effect of his words. With numb detachment, she noticed her neckline was gaping, showing the full upper curve of her breasts. Hastily, she rearranged her dress, thankful her hair had loosened enough to cover the heat rushing into her face.

She sensed him coming closer. For a second she thought he would touch her, soothe away his harshly spoken words, but when she risked a glance she saw him veer towards the door.

Anger, gratefully received in place of fruitless hope, roiled through her. She surged to her feet and yanked her dress down.

'Why?'

He didn't turn around.

'Tell me why you still wear your wedding ring but are condemning our marriage?' She heard the strained bewilderment in her voice and would have given her eye teeth not to. 'Is it…is it because you don't love me any more?'

With one hand tensed on the doorknob, he turned. 'Any more?'

'Yes. Is that it?'

'Ava, I desired you. I craved you with a need and desperation that bordered on the unholy. But I never claimed to love you.'

Ava lay in darkness, sleep a thousand miles away as Cesare's words played an unrelenting refrain in her head. Words that had cut into her, devastated her so completely that she'd sunk into the sofa, incapable of speech.

Cesare, of course, had walked out after reminding her coolly of their call to Celine the next day. She'd clamped her lips together, begging whatever fates were within hearing distance to help her hold it together until he was out of earshot.

Then a long, hideous whimper had escaped her. The sound had reminded her of a wounded animal, alien and ugly, torn from the depths of her soul.

In that moment she'd hated herself. She'd always been weak when it came to Cesare. Minutes after meeting him, and agreeing to have a drink with him at a wine bar in London, she'd known in a deep, innate part of her being that he possessed the power to make her do things, *feel* things no other human being could. They'd never made it to the wine bar. He'd taken her to his country pad in Surrey and they'd ended up making love, right there on the bonnet of his car in the middle of his driveway. It had been the start of the most erotic, soul-shaking six weeks of her life.

Yes, he'd enthralled her from the very first look.

But the sex wasn't why she'd fallen for Cesare. During those six weeks, he'd taken care of her, treated her as if she was the most important thing in his life. And for someone who'd always felt like an afterthought in her family, it'd been like being handed a little piece of heaven.

Ava turned over, punched her frustration into her pillow. For Cesare to deny the man he'd been before their marriage and Annabelle's birth hurt her deeply. Because that man had been there—she hadn't dreamed him. Or had she?

She sucked in a shaky breath. Cesare's accusation that she was pushy, of foisting her dreams on him, cut through her muddled thoughts like deadly acid.

Falling pregnant with Annabelle so soon after meeting Cesare had merely accelerated the realisation of a lifelong desire, because nurturing a family she could call her own had always been her one and only dream. And when Cesare had proposed, she'd thought it'd been his dream too.

How wrong she'd been.

Because, she recalled, for a split second after she'd told him she was pregnant, Cesare had looked like a man who'd just glimpsed his worst nightmare.

'But we were so careful. How could this have happened?' he'd asked in shaken disbelief.

Since she'd asked herself that very same question, but with a burgeoning joy, she couldn't have summoned an answer to save her life.

Ava threw back the covers and padded to the window. Moonlight gleamed off the courtyard flagstones—the same flagstones she'd stood on when Cesare had proposed.

I never claimed to love you.

Foolish tears prickled her eyes. She wanted to hate Cesare for his callous words, but he was right. He'd never said the words. Oh, he'd demonstrated his desire exceptionally well; he'd provided for her every carnal and materialistic wish. But he'd never told her he loved her. She'd just...*assumed*...

Damn it. She wouldn't cry. Hell, at the back of her mind she'd accepted that at some point one of them would have to make a move to dissolve this empty marriage.

Except, of course, when the time had come she hadn't demanded a separation or divorce. She'd practically begged for him to take her back.

How pathetic was she? Furious with herself for wallowing in self-pity, she threw a shirt over her thigh-length nightgown, grabbed the monitor and left her suite.

Aimlessly wandering the house, she finally ended up in the kitchen. A wry smile twisted her lips. Her brother, Nathan, the only one of her three brothers who'd come remotely close to acknowledging her existence when they were growing up, would have mocked her mercilessly if he'd seen she'd reverted to her old habit of comfort-eating. Opening the fridge, she took out a half bottle of Soave and poured herself a glass.

A small platter of *stromboli* stood next to the

large stove. She picked one and bit into it, then, on impulse, she tugged the phone off the wall, dialled her brother's number. Her disappointment was tinged with relief when she got his voicemail.

What would she have said to him anyway? That her husband had announced he'd never loved her and a part of her believed she'd caused her marriage breakdown by forcing a family? Grimacing, she left a short, nondescript message and hung up.

She turned and jumped at the shadow looming in the doorway. Her heart flipped several times more when Cesare stepped into the subdued kitchen light.

'*Mi dispiace*. I heard voices.' His narrowed glance went to the phone, then returned to her. 'Who were you calling at this time of the night?' he demanded.

'Nathan. I got his voicemail. I was leaving a message.'

'Have any of your family been in touch recently?'

'You mean have they developed a desperate need to get to know the sister they've rejected all their lives? That would be a no.' She refused to acknowledge the pain.

Cesare frowned. 'Do they know what's happened to you this past month?'

She swallowed the lump in her throat. 'They

don't concern themselves with my well-being, Cesare. They never have.'

'I'm sorry—'

'I don't need you to be. And I don't need your pity. What I need you won't give me, so you can either leave me in peace, or we can change the subject.'

He stared at her for a full minute, then he leaned against the doorjamb. His gaze slid over her, lingering in places it had no right to linger. She wanted to scream at him to stop looking at her. But this was Cesare. Asking wouldn't mean getting.

Silence stretched as neither made a move to speak. The air in the open space closed off, growing thick until it felt as if they breathed the same pocket of oxygen.

Slowly, excitement licked through her belly, transmitting knee-weakening desire along her nerve endings. Ava forced herself to remember. Remembering how she'd humiliated herself a mere two hours ago fortified her resolve. She moved forward, then paused, realising that to walk out of the door she'd have to go past him.

Her glance fell to his hands and took in white padding and red specks where his knuckles bled. 'You've been in the gym?'

Cesare kept a fully equipped gym in all of his homes and kept ultra-fit by boxing.

He gave a grim nod. 'I was overwhelmed by the need to pummel something.' His eyes locked on hers, drilling into her until she feared he could see right through her.

'How did that work out for you?' Her voice emerged breathless, strained. She took a hasty sip of her wine.

'Not nearly as successful as I'd hoped it would. You?'

'I leave the pummelling to others.' She raised the items in her hand. 'I prefer to wage my war armed with carbs and wine. I'll let you know later if I'm winning.'

Half of her had hoped her answer would drive him away. The other half, the foolish half that never listened to reason where Cesare was concerned, leaped with joy when he came closer, slowly unwinding the padding from his bound fingers. Sweat glistened off his honed biceps, emphasising the play of superb muscle as he moved. Even more riveting was his half smile, more potent now he'd stopped beside her.

'Pour me a glass, would you?' He nodded at her glass.

'Do you think it's a good idea?'

He surveyed her with the sleepy regard of a jungle predator. The taut smile that barely curved his lips was acutely discerning. 'For me to drink wine, or for us to be in the same room at the same time?'

'Both.' She cursed her candid tongue and tried to address the less volatile issue. 'Also, isn't water the recommended drink after hectic exercise?'

Heat flared in her cheeks as his gaze turned even more intense. The torrid promise of sheet-burning sex pulsed between them. His nostrils flared for a second before he moved to the sink and ran his hands under the tap.

'I drank water after the workout. Now I need something…stronger.' His gaze dropped to her chest, his bold stare causing her breasts to grow heavier. 'I'll get the wine myself if you can't stand to be here.'

The clear challenge made her bolder. The red in her hair and nature made backing down from a challenge an impossibility—or so she'd often been told.

She wouldn't slink away like a scared puppy just because Cesare was in a testy mood. Setting her drink on the vast centre island, she pulled out a stool and perched on it.

Cesare grabbed a glass, brought over the plate of *stromboli* and placed it down between them. She poured his wine as he took a bite of bread. After taking a sip, he sat back and looked at her.

'Sleep was eluding you also?'

'I think sleep would elude any woman whose husband announces he never loved her and regrets marrying her.'

He tensed immediately. 'Ava—'

'It's okay. No, actually, it's not okay but I'm not about to launch into another bout of hysteria if that's what you're worried about.'

He exhaled. 'You're the last woman I'd accuse of hysterics. But *grazie.*'

The piece of pastry she popped into her mouth to delay her response tasted like sawdust with a hint of garlic. Taking another sip of wine helped her force it down, but realising another bite wasn't a good idea because she risked choking, she put it down.

'Don't thank me just yet. I'm still reeling from the revelations about Roberto and about us. Just because I'm calm now doesn't mean we don't have a situation that doesn't need to be resolved.' Clearing her throat, she forced the words out. 'I think it's time we stop playing ostrich and take what's happening between us to the next…permanent level.'

The violent scrape of the stool as he pushed it

back on the tiled floor raked across nerves already raw with her ravaged emotions.

Cesare planted both hands on the smooth surface and glared fire and brimstone at her. 'Di Goias do not divorce.'

Her mouth fell open. *'Excuse me?* Shouldn't you have thought of that before you decided to enter a marriage you didn't want?'

'You were carrying my child. I had no choice.' His lips barely moved with his words.

She sucked in a stunned breath. 'Wow, you do know how to keep piling on the charm, don't you? I'm sure you would've made some damsel a perfect husband in the Dark Ages. Unfortunately for you, we're in the twenty-first century, so unless I signed on to this *Di Goias Do Not Divorce* without knowing about it, I don't see that you have a choice.'

His glare intensified. 'You knew we were only marrying because of Annabelle.'

'Wrong! I thought you were marrying me because you loved me, that you wanted to make a *family* with me.'

He stepped back abruptly as if she'd physically assaulted him. 'Again with the family!'

'What is so wrong with that?' she yelled, suddenly not feeling so calm any more.

'I never confessed such a feeling.'

'I know. Stupid me, mistranslating all those heated Italian endearments you whispered to me in bed as words of devotion and undying love.'

A dull flush washed across his taut cheekbones. 'I never lied to you about my feelings in or out of bed.'

'But you made me think you cared about me, that you wanted what I wanted. It was a lie by omission.'

As if frustrated with her logic, he whirled away from the island and started pacing in tight circles. She followed his prowl, helpless to avert her gaze because Cesare had always been a source of intense, almost worshipful fascination for her.

He finally returned and gripped the edge of the countertop. 'I never lied to you, Ava. And I did care.' His gaze speared hers, almost imploring, as if he willed her to believe him.

She swallowed. 'Obviously not enough. Ultimately, it was all about the sex for you. Shame I had to go and get pregnant, wasn't it?' The words were forced through a painful knot in her throat. 'Whatever you say next, even if you think and feel it, please do not tell me you regret having our daughter.'

Pain flitted over his face. In the next instant it

was gone. 'I have not for a single moment regretted Annabelle. But you have to admit, things got very complicated very quickly with us.'

She released the breath locked in her throat and quickly swallowed down the threatening tears.

Enough.

Before she got sucked down into a quagmire of her own making, she stood. 'Well, it's time to *de-complicate* things. There's nothing to stop me seeking a divorce so whether you want one or not doesn't really matter. You said you shouldn't have married me, that I was too fixated on wanting a family with you to see that you didn't want one. I hate you for misleading me if that's the way you really felt. You still want me—do us both a favour and don't deny it, please. You want me but you don't want to be married to me, and yet you still wear your wedding ring.

'Frankly, I don't have a clue what's going on, but I'm done turning myself into a basket case trying to figure it out. So I don't really give a damn if it's the *di Goia thing* or not, Cesare. I want a divorce.'

CHAPTER SIX

CESARE DESCENDED THE stairs, his mood no less foul than when he'd gone upstairs three hours earlier under the pretext of going to bed.

Sleep had been non-existent. No surprise there. Irrational anger and frustration pulsed in equal measures through him. For the most part he was extremely disturbed by his reaction to Ava's announcement in the kitchen. Which in turn confused him. He was not a man who enjoyed being confused!

And yet, what had he expected when he announced they shouldn't have married? That she would dissolve in helpless tears and beg him to reconsider?

He gave a grim smile. Ava was not like that. No, his redheaded tigress reacted with claws, not tears. But there'd been no signs of claws last night... only a calm resignation after her hysterics-free announcement.

The disturbing hollowness inside him expanded.

Even if some masochistic part of him had wanted her to fight, what good would it have done? He wasn't wired to be a family man. He never would be.

Di Goias do not divorce. He snorted under his breath. For a man who prided himself on being ruthlessly straight in his business dealings, he was sure as hell making a pathetic ass of himself in his private life.

Ava only needed a competent Internet search engine to verify his hot-headed statement as a pack of lies. Granted, divorce in his family was rare, but wasn't his Uncle Gianni neck-deep in a particularly messy one with his third wife right this very minute?

Cesare slammed the door to his study and paced the room. A dark part of him registered his anger was irrational. As irrational as the fear he'd felt when he'd had to leave Ava and Annabelle three weeks ago to rush to Roberto's side. Then, as now, he'd felt as if his life was ripping apart with the same deadly intent as the earthquake had.

He detested the hellish, out-of-control feeling.

The past weeks' events—the earthquake, Roberto's death, the soul-shaking despair of not being able to control anything in life had only cemented his belief that he shouldn't have married Ava.

So why should he be angry now that she wanted out?

'Basta!' he swore under his breath. Glancing at his watch, he stalked to the phone. It was still early on a Saturday morning, and it was about time his lawyers earned their fat monthly retainer.

'Ciao!'

Cesare pulled the phone from his ear, surprise spiking through him when he realised whose number he'd dialled.

'Buon giorno, Celine.'

'You sound surprised even though *you* called *me.*' Her bewilderment matched his.

'Perdono, I was calling someone else,' he said.

Celine's laugh was a little strained. 'Maybe it's Fate forcing us to finish last night's conversation.'

He sighed. 'I've told her. She knows everything.'

'Oh, I'm so glad, Cesare. I allowed Roberto to push me away and I'll never forgive myself for not being there for him until it was almost too late. We barely got a chance to say goodbye before he was gone. I'm glad you're not making the same mistake…' Her voice broke.

Pain tightened in his chest before he forcefully hardened his emotions. He wasn't in the mood to enlighten Celine that he and wife couldn't be further apart if they tried. 'I appreciate what you did for Roberto, just as I appreciate what you're doing for my fam—for me. *Ciao*, Celine.' He quickly ended the call and threw the phone on his desk.

His jaw tightened against the helplessness that dogged him and he had the feeling Fate wasn't done with him yet.

Closing his eyes, he tried to clear his head but there was no erasing his mind's fixation on a particular woman. A woman with hair the colour of a glorious Tuscany sunset, peach-perfect skin dusted with freckles as countless as the stars. Emerald-green eyes that sucked him into seductive pools in which he wanted to happily drown.

The arousal that had plagued him since she returned throbbed to life, an insistent beat of desire that pounded through his system like a relentless drumbeat.

It would all go away. He just needed the right focus. One call on Monday to his lawyers to set divorce proceedings underway and this feeling would go away.

Satisfied that he'd regained some control, he left the study.

Lucia was laying out the breakfast things and turned at his approach. The usually stern face of the woman who'd been part of his household for longer than he could remember relaxed into a smile as she regaled him with Annabelle's antics of the day before.

Cesare had noted the change in his household since his daughter's return. The household staff who normally went out of their way to avoid him now smiled openly and even exchanged greetings instead of hurrying away when they saw him coming.

As he poured himself a coffee, he admitted to the lightness in his own heart since Annabelle's return. But there was also a stab of pain so acute his hand shook. He'd almost lost her once. He had no intention of doing so again.

She was the only child he would bear; she would one day inherit the di Goia fortune. Which meant she had to be prepared. And, for starters, a daughter who spoke more English than Italian was simply unacceptable.

'You look like you're plotting world domination.'

Ava stood framed in the terrace doorway, dressed in a short white sundress. The sight of her long bare legs sent volcanic heat surging through his veins.

Sunlight flamed hair brightened by the Balinese sun. Her fair skin never browned enough to tan, but it glowed with a healthy hue and shimmered as if she'd smoothed a special lotion over it.

He watched her glide on bare feet towards him. In all the time he'd known Ava, he'd only seen her wear shoes when they went out and, even then, at the earliest opportunity she kicked them off. Instruments of torture, she called them. He'd never objected because he found her unadorned feet extremely sexy. He'd never have imagined he had a foot fetish before he met her.

But then he was equally fascinated with her fingers, with her lips, with the delicate bones of her clavicle and the sweet temptation of her round, supple breasts.

Madre di Dio! he cursed as his insane desire for her rose to torment him again.

Hips swaying beneath the soft, clingy material, she reached the table, chose the chair next to him and folded herself into it. Immediately the subtle scent of her perfume hit his nostrils, sending desire surging higher.

'Should I be afraid?' Her voice was a husky rasp in his ears. He had to concentrate hard to remember what she'd said.

He forced a smile. 'I am plotting, *cara*, but not world domination. What I desire is much smaller, but no less important.'

Unease entered her eyes but she tried to mask it. When she looked away and poured her tea, he couldn't resist the irrational urge to tease her, to pay her back for the suffering he endured. Hell, he knew it wasn't her fault that he found her so alluring, so damned beautiful that all he wanted to do was bury the stiff, pulsing part of himself inside her, but he felt rattled enough not to heed caution's voice.

'Don't you want to know what it is?' he asked softly.

The teapot shook and she set it down. That small betrayal was quickly masked because when she glanced at him the deep endless pools of her eyes were clear and calm. But they still drew him in like a siren's call.

'Not particularly, but I get the feeling you're in a sharing mood.'

He smiled. 'I am indeed. Annabelle doesn't speak any Italian.'

Her eyes widened. 'What?'

'My daughter does not speak Italian.'

Her eyes flashed. 'And whose fault is that? English is *my* first language, not Italian.'

'But you have a great handle on Italian. Or at least you did when we were together.'

She shrugged and he cursed himself for being

distracted by the delicate movement of her shoulder. 'Since I seem to have misinterpreted so much of what you said to me in Italian, maybe I didn't have as great a handle on the language as I thought.'

He deserved that but it didn't make him seethe any less. 'I want her to learn my language.'

To his surprise, she nodded. 'I don't have any objection. Lucia is already teaching her. She's a very quick study. I'm sure she'll pick it up easily enough.'

Her easy capitulation unsettled him even further. Seeing his reaction, she shrugged again. 'I'm determined to be hysteria-free from now on, Cesare. Deal with it.'

'Deal with it?' He wasn't sure why that particular statement made him angrier.

'Do you mind taking care of Annabelle this morning? I know we're supposed to spend weekends with her but I need to check out the lighting for the blessing in the church and the caretaker can only make today.'

'Where is this church?' he bit out.

'The Duomo in Amalfi.'

'I'll drive you there.'

'There's no need.'

He set his coffee down. '*Sì*, there's every need. If

we all go together then we don't break the agreement to spend time with our daughter. Where is she, by the way?'

'She took a detour to the kitchen to ask Lucia to put blueberries in her pancakes. But—'

Before she could protest further about his decision to drive into Amalfi with her, Annabelle flew onto the terrace, her hair streaming behind her like a fast-flowing river. His heart caught with joy, then sang with pride when she greeted him in halting Italian.

'*Buon giorno, piccolina,*' he responded, trying to keep his voice steady.

Ava watched the play of emotion on Cesare's face as he lifted Annabelle onto his lap for a kiss. Another sliver of unease darted through her. On the surface, Cesare's request that Annabelle learn Italian had seemed innocuous. But she couldn't dismiss the anxiety that settled in her stomach like a lead balloon.

Was she blowing everything out of proportion, just like she'd blown her importance to Cesare out of proportion? Maybe Cesare was being exactly what he claimed—an Italian father with the natural urge to speak his language with his child.

Her fingers stilled on the banana she was peeling

for Annabelle and she watched father and daughter converse—one voice a deep, gravelly tone, the other a childish but attentive copying that filled her heart with equal measures of pride and pain.

As if sensing her gaze, Cesare glanced up.

The breath left her lungs and her heart careened around her ribcage like a crazed animal seeking freedom.

Even after Annabelle grabbed her banana and settled in her seat to munch on it, he continued to stare at her. Heat arced between them, just like it had from the very first time they'd met.

Once again the stinging betrayal of her need echoed between her legs. A helpless moan escaped her before she quickly disguised it as a cough.

His eyes darkened nevertheless.

'Stop it,' she muttered fiercely.

He raised an eyebrow and shrugged. 'Can't help it.'

'Try harder!' Or she was scared she'd spontaneously combust the way her pulse was skittering out of control.

Tawny eyes narrowed. 'Is that an order?'

'It's a friendly health warning.'

His smile was pure male arrogance, his gaze unwavering as he sipped his coffee.

'My parents wish to see Annabelle. I also have a

few meetings in Rome, so it would be a good time to make it happen.'

'How are they coping with…' she paused, her glance sliding to Annabelle '…with what happened to Roberto?'

A flash of pain passed over Cesare's face, his eyes straying to Annabelle. 'As most parents would, I expect.' His gaze returned to Ava. 'They need not know about our…situation just yet. I don't want them upset.'

Ava abandoned the pretence of eating and tucked a strand of hair behind her ear. 'They know we've lived apart for a year, Cesare.'

'But my mother assumes since we're both here, living under the same roof that we've resolved our differences. Once the summer is over, we'll update them on what they need to know.'

Against her will, but because she didn't want to cause any further distress to newly bereaved parents, she nodded. 'When were you thinking of going to Rome?' Annabelle's grandparents doted on her and she'd never deny Orsini and Carmela di Goia the chance to see their granddaughter.

'Monday morning. I have meetings in the afternoon.'

'How long will you be gone?'

He drained his coffee. 'If you agree, Annabelle

will spend the night with my parents on Monday. I'll pick her up on Tuesday and we'll return on Wednesday.'

'Two nights…' She would miss her child but the time away would help her put her feelings regarding Cesare into some sort of perspective.

Being constantly around him, waging a seemingly hopeless battle with her feelings had become draining. In a way, this was a blessing in disguise.

The time would also be useful for a drive down to Amalfi to scout out some more locations for the wedding catalogue.

She tried not to be distracted by the play of his hair-dusted bicep as he reached over and plucked a peach from the bowl. 'I suppose two nights isn't so bad. Is Lucia coming with you?'

'No, she isn't.'

She frowned. 'I don't think it's a good idea—'

'You think I'm incapable of taking care of our child?' A hard glint entered his eyes, chilling the skin on her arms.

'It's not that,' she answered truthfully.

'Then what is it?'

'Annabelle can be a handful, especially when she gets tired. I just think it's a good idea to have some help, that's all.'

'Which is why you're coming with us,' he said.

'*Me?* But I wasn't—I didn't…'

'Wasn't that the agreement? We spend every day with our daughter?'

'Yes, but what about my work? I have a meeting with Reynaldo and Tina on Monday morning.'

He frowned. 'What time will you be done?'

'About eleven.'

'*Bene*, we'll leave at midday.' He turned to his daughter. 'If you want a swim with *Papà* after breakfast, then go easy on those pancakes, *piccola mia*.'

'Will you swim too, Mummy?' her daughter asked.

'Yes, she will,' Cesare answered for her. 'Mummy is not in any danger because she's barely eaten a thing.' His disapproving gaze moved from her barely touched plate to her face, and challenged her to refute his words.

The discreet but extremely rude finger gesture she used in his direction produced an amused smile. Then his gaze released hers to travel at leisure down her face to the frantic pulse beating at her throat.

Unable to stand the sensual heat any more, she set back her chair and stood.

'I'll just go and change.' As she walked away,

a saucy thought entered her head. Since she'd got here, Cesare had teased and taunted her sexually.

Well, two could play that game.

In her room, she quickly selected her skimpiest bikini, one bought for her trip to Bali when she'd been under the delusion that she could save her marriage.

She tried it on now and nearly lost her nerve. The bright green Lycra material—where there was any—clung to her skin in a blatantly provocative caress.

Flushing, she pulled a matching green shirt over it, grabbed a bottle of sun protection and hurried out of the room before she changed her mind. With each step towards the pool, she reiterated to herself the purpose of her actions.

She'd never been a pushover. On the contrary, she'd learned very early on in life to push back when pushed. Cesare had pushed her buttons enough.

The moment she shrugged off her shirt and caught his gaze, her heartbeat screamed out of control. Where sexual heat had burned lazily in his eyes before, this time they blazed with pure volcanic heat. The sheer power of it made her stumble to a halt. Heat rushed up and engulfed her whole body. Uncertain, she stood at the edge of the pool.

Cesare's face set into hardened lines. His nostrils were pinched and his jaw was clamped tight as if holding himself by a bare thread. He couldn't have made it plainer that she'd succeeded in pushing him to his very limit.

She wanted to run as fast as she could back to her room, tear the bikini off and burn the damned thing. But she couldn't move. Concrete-heavy limbs remained riveted to the tiles, her whole body drenched in a need so strong it took her breath away.

His gaze slid downward, his expression growing tighter as it travelled over her and back to her face.

Finally, he turned to his daughter, made sure her armbands were secured, then he swam to the side of the pool.

In one vault he was beside her. 'What the hell are you trying to do to me?'

She fought to hold a smile in place. 'Payback's a bitch, isn't it?'

He stared down at her, and then proceeded to circle her. When he reached her back, she heard a harshly drawn breath.

Despite her intentions, she cringed at the sound because she knew what he was seeing. Three fragile lines barely held the bikini together. It would take little more than a tug for it to disintegrate.

'*Santa Maria.* You've never played this dirty before,' he croaked.

'I'm...sorry?'

'You're *not* sorry. You're trying to punish me, make me want you so badly, I can't see straight.' His mouth was next to her ear, his breath hot against her skin.

Heat fired through her but she refused to back down. 'I'm merely playing your game, Cesare. Question is, what are you going to do about it?'

He gripped her arms and whirled her to face him. 'You want me to demonstrate the thousand different ways I want you? Now, in front of our daughter?'

'I—' Words failed her as shame racked through her. This wasn't the outcome she'd wished for when she'd brazenly flung on the costume. 'I didn't mean to—'

'You wanted to make me suffer, *sì*? Consider yourself successful. I'm burning for you, Ava. Make no mistake about that.'

Helplessly, she shook her head.

Without warning, his lips captured her lobe and he bit her less than gently. She barely managed to smother her gasp as hot darts of desire pelted her from head to toe. But, before she could completely melt under his assault, he'd released her.

By the time she'd opened her eyes, her shirt, warm from the sun, was once again around her shoulders. Cesare stood behind her until she'd folded her arms into them.

She started to move away but he grabbed her waist.

'Are you satisfied now? Are you pleased with your little *experiment*?' He pulled her back against him. The solid imprint of his arousal burned hot against her back. This time she couldn't suppress her moan. But it was a moan of frustration and regret because she knew, much as she'd wanted him to suffer, she'd only succeeded in prolonging her own suffering.

'Yes,' she managed to say.

'Good, because this is as far as you're ever going to get, Ava.'

Her heart cracked and her legs threatened to give way. 'Why? Have you developed a premature ejaculation problem?' she mocked, unwilling to concede defeat despite every atom in her body wanting to slink away in shame.

Cesare gave a husky laugh. 'Far from it, *bella,*' he taunted, even as he pressed himself closer. 'But you want a divorce, remember? So, technically, my hard-ons no longer belong to you. Think about that the next time you decide to test the fires so brazenly, *tesoro mio.*'

With supreme effort, she snatched herself from his arms. She stumbled a few steps before stopping to drag air into her lungs. When she was certain she could stand without collapsing, she tugged the folds of the shirt together. Her fingers shook too hard to button it, so she just held it with one hand.

When she risked a glance at Cesare, he'd wrapped a large towel around his waist and now sat on the edge of a sun lounger, his eyes tracking his daughter as she exhibited her newly learned crawl. His fists were bunched tight on his thighs and his breathing was shallow, as if he'd run a marathon.

Without a word, she turned and went inside as fast as her legs could carry her. The bikini ripped as she tugged it off. Staring at the garment in her shaking hands, she felt a huge lump wedge in her throat.

She'd pushed them both to the limit. And what had that proved? They were still as hot as hell for each other…and? *And nothing.*

Hot sex could never sustain a marriage that had been doomed from the beginning. Deep down, she knew that.

Ava sank onto the side of the bed and finally admitted to herself the reason why she'd felt the need to test his resolve.

Her marriage was well and truly dead. It was time to accept it.

CHAPTER SEVEN

ROME IN JULY was a seething, vibrant mass of sensible locals who sought shade and tourists who defiantly basked in the rapidly soaring temperatures. Ensconced in the limo heading towards the restaurant where they were meeting Cesare's parents, Ava was grateful for the air-conditioner. What she wasn't safe from were the thoughts reverberating in her head.

This is as far as you're ever going to get.

She tried to push the haunting words away. They pounded harder, bringing with them a dreadful sinking in her stomach. When her phone buzzed, she pounced on it, only to frown as she saw the text sender.

'It's Agata Marinello again. She's whining about your continued silence. Why don't you just tell her you won't be attending the wedding and be done with it so I can have a bit of peace? Or am I so far in the dog house you can't even be bothered to find the key and let me out?'

Cesare looked up from the electronic tablet he'd been working on since they'd transferred from helicopter to car.

'Why would you be in the dog house?' His voice was coolly neutral.

Her fingers tightened around her phone. 'Really, are we going to play this game?'

'No, there will be no more games, *cara*. I think we've reached an understanding on where we both stand. Finally.' His cool demeanour was nothing like the held-together-by-a-thread aroused male he'd been at the pool.

He'd picked her up from her meeting dressed in a custom-made suit, polished shoes, sunglasses in place, looking intoxicatingly magnificent, as always.

After seeing him in casual clothes every day for almost two weeks, the sight of him dressed for business, his dynamic persona in place, only made her agitation worse.

The short drive down to the helipad and the flight into Rome been accomplished in near silence, save for Annabelle's chatter.

'You intend to freeze me out for the foreseeable future? That's fine. But can you find half a minute and text Agata and tell her you're not attending her precious son's wedding? Because her texts are seriously driving me insane. And I won't be accountable for my actions if she keeps it up,' she warned.

He shot her a hooded, speculative look before he nodded. 'I'll get in touch with her before the close of play today.'

'Thank you. You can go back to ignoring me now.'

After checking Annabelle still dozed in her car seat, she stared out of the window as the car edged around the Trevi Fountain and headed west towards Campo de Fiori.

His tablet pinged as he shut it off. She knew the moment he turned to stare at her, the weight of his gaze so heavy, anxiety ratcheted several notches higher.

'Ava—'

'I'm sorry, okay?'

He stiffened, his fingers tightening around the stylus he'd been working with.

Pain settled in her chest as she recalled how those hands had felt on her, once upon a time. How spellbindingly erotic they could be.

A car horn blasted, making him turn momentarily to glance out of the window. Sunlight glinted off his black mane, casting it a glossy blue-black. His profile, stunning and powerful, hit her in the solar plexus, causing her breath to lodge in her lungs. She didn't know why she was surprised by her reaction.

Cesare, even with the slightly crooked nose sustained during a boxing match in his youth, was as close to physical perfection as any man could get. The urge to touch him made her fists clench until her nails bit into her palms. Sitting this close to him and stopping herself from touching was pure torture.

For a second, she regretted not insisting on staying in Lake Como. She glanced at him again and considered returning to the villa.

Wuss.

'I'm sorry,' she forced out again. 'I know I get rash at times. The pool incident…I don't know what I was thinking.'

His gaze flicked to Annabelle, and then back to her once he'd assured himself she still napped. 'I do, and I'm sorry too,' he said with a sigh. 'Sex—or the promise of it—has become our fall-back solution to what's happening between us. I used it to teach you a lesson the day you returned. You returned the favour yesterday and I deserved it. We've been pushing each other relentlessly. One of us was bound to reach boiling point eventually.'

'And of course it had to be me.'

'No. I haven't been fair to you, Ava. The earthquake shook all of us out of our complacency. And losing Roberto…' His jaw clenched.

Uncurling her hand, she placed it over his and felt momentary warmth flow between them. 'When will we find out what happened to Roberto?'

His eyes darkened. 'Soon…' He stopped when his phone rang but he ignored it and pinched the bridge of his nose. 'We're almost at the restaurant. After that, I have meetings. We'll talk some more tonight. Okay?'

Her heart climbed into her throat but she forced a nod. 'Okay.'

With a long deep breath, he pulled out his phone. *'Ciao.'* His smooth, husky voice echoed in the air-conditioned car.

She tensed when a female voice returned the greeting. The rapid flow of Italian was too much for her to follow, but her tension escalated as he spoke in low, intimate tones.

Ava's fists tightened further when he settled back and made himself more comfortable. The movement brought him closer, his powerful thigh brushing hers as he widened his legs. She was trying to shift away from the torturous contact when he turned and held out the phone.

'Celine wishes to speak to you.'

She drew in a quick breath. 'Why?'

He shrugged. 'We never got round to making that phone call. I tried to apologise on your behalf but she wants to make sure there are no bad feelings.'

She snatched the phone from him and placed her palm over the speaker. 'How dare you apologise on my behalf? I'm not some child whose behaviour has to be excused.'

He regarded her coolly. 'Well, this is your chance. You can hang up or you can speak to her. Your choice.'

Futile irritation welled up inside her. 'God, I really hate you sometimes.'

He merely smiled.

She cleared her throat and removed her hand. 'Celine, hello.'

'*Ciao*, Ava,' she answered. Her tone was warm, totally devoid of censure, which made Ava feel worse.

'Look, I'm sorry about the other night...' As she made her apologies, it occurred to her that she'd made a lot of them in the last hour.

'...being married to a man like Cesare would make any woman guard her place in his heart. He's very special.'

The arrogant upward curve of his mouth told her Cesare had heard Celine's words.

'He's also stubborn and extremely infuriating,' Ava muttered.

Celine laughed. 'You won't hear any arguments from me. But his heart is in the right place. Please remember that.'

The vehemence in Celine's tone made Ava frown. She watched Cesare put his tablet away and couldn't look away from the elegant hand he rested on his thighs. The memory of those hands on her skin hit her sideways. Her fingers clenched around the phone; Celine's words were lost in a jumble as heat surged through her.

She glanced up to find Cesare's eyes on her. Unable to pull her gaze away, she pressed her lips together to stop them tingling. After a few seconds his eyes flicked to the phone, his brow raised.

Celine was calling her name. Embarrassed, she apologized—again—then forced herself to conduct a somewhat coherent conversation. Minutes later, she gratefully disconnected the call.

Cesare laughed under his breath.

'Smugness is an unattractive trait,' she snapped, her voice disgustingly husky from the feelings rampaging through her.

His smile only widened. 'But it does my heart good to watch you eat humble pie,' he returned.

'Well, before I dig in, you should know I've accepted an invitation for Celine's birthday tonight.' She named the club. 'She's texting me the details shortly.'

His smile disappeared. Cesare hated nightclubs.

With a satisfied smile of her own, she held out his phone. 'Not so smug now, huh, *caro?*'

Cesare let himself into his apartment just before seven that evening and was immediately struck by the silence. It was different from this afternoon, when the sound of Annabelle's laughter coupled with Ava's huskier laugh had bounced off the walls. Realising how badly he missed it, he dropped his briefcase and loosened his tie.

Nothing was going according to plan. The business he'd thought he would have concluded by mid-afternoon today had stretched well into the evening. He knew his lack of concentration had been mostly to blame. He hadn't missed the surreptitious glances his board executives had exchanged when they'd thought he wasn't aware.

How could they know he was dreading the next few hours? This was the first time he'd be alone—

truly alone—with Ava. And he didn't trust himself one iota.

Stalking to the cabinet, he plucked a glass from the shelf and contemplated the extensive array of drinks. He poured a shot of cognac, knocked it back and slammed the glass down.

Get a grip!

He eyed his briefcase. Part of the answer to his problems lay in there. All he had to do was sign the divorce papers his lawyers had drawn up and Ava would be out of his life.

He stepped forward and stopped when something soft gave way underfoot. Bending down, he picked up Annabelle's teddy. With a pang, he clutched the toy and clenched his gut against the pain shooting through him.

He loved his child beyond imagining, and yet he'd never been able to celebrate that love without a heavy dose of guilt. How could he when his actions had deprived Roberto of the same joy of being a father?

Cesare placed the teddy on the table. A sound behind him made him turn.

Ava stood at the entrance to the hallway, dressed in a long satin robe, her freshly washed and shining hair falling over one shoulder in an innocently seductive gesture that made his head swim. His chest tightened and he forced himself to remain still, to fight the urge to drag her close, imprison that trim waist and devour her lips with his.

'I thought I heard someone in here.' She moved into the room. As hard as he fought, he couldn't stop his gaze straying to the sensual sway of her hips.

His whole body tautened so tight he was sure he'd snap in two.

Santa cielo! A year without sex was messing with his mind. Only monks took perpetual vows of celibacy. And his body was reminding him in the most elemental, primitive way possible that *he* was no monk.

He turned away to hide his growing hard-on.

'I just got in. Did my parents get away with Annabelle okay?'

Her robe whispered as she came closer. He closed his eyes. Before long her scent would reach him. Mingled dread and fierce anticipation scythed through him.

'Yes.' He heard the smile in her voice. 'I'm not sure which one of them was more excited. Their plans for tomorrow exhausted me and all I did was listen to them.'

'She left her teddy.' He needed to fill the silence or give in to the urge to touch her.

'Hmm, I know. I called Carmela and offered to take it over but she said no. I think I handed her the perfect excuse to take Annabelle shopping for another one.'

Unable to resist any longer, he turned. Her smile was breathtaking. *Dio mio, everything about her was breathtaking.* Shoving one hand through his hair, he pulled his tie away completely with the other.

'What time is Celine's thing?' Getting out of here might help with this unrelenting obsession to keep checking out his future ex-wife.

'Eight o'clock for drinks and dinner, then on to the club.'

He grimaced. The last thing he wanted was to socialise to the beat of thumping music. But anywhere else was preferable to being cooped up in this apartment, alone with Ava and his shockingly impure thoughts.

'Give me twenty minutes to shower and change.'

Her fingers toyed with the knot in her robe belt. He directed his gaze elsewhere.

'I'd hoped you'd return earlier. You said we needed to talk?' she ventured.

'I'm sorry, I was delayed. Unavoid—' He stopped when her smile dimmed. 'We don't have to stay long at Celine's party. We'll talk when we get back, *sì*?'

Her lips firmed. 'We'd better. The suspense is killing me.'

Twenty minutes later, he was seriously contemplating calling off the evening. But he knew he'd never hear the end of it if he disappointed Celine.

Grimly, he slid silver cufflinks into his black silk shirt, shrugged on his dinner jacket and emerged from his room just as Ava shut the door to the guest room.

His couldn't describe the miasma of emotions that fizzed through him.

The emerald-green thigh-length sheath she wore had no back. He knew this because her skin was exhibited in soft, gleaming peach-perfect invitation.

'Are you missing something?' His voice sounded strained even to his own ears.

She performed a perfect pirouette and then stared wide-eyed at him. The tingle of satisfaction he felt that she still found him attractive disappeared underneath the seething idea of other men seeing her in that piece of nothing.

She made a show of touching her fingers to the diamond studs in her lobes and the stylish pendant around her throat before checking the silver open-toed heels on her feet.

'No, I think I'm all set.' Her hair gleamed in the light as she raised her gaze to his.

'Are you sure, because you look stunning, but I think you're missing several yards of material at the back of your dress.'

Despite the surge of blood reddening her cheeks, she raised an eyebrow. 'Oh, and suddenly you care how I look, Cesare?'

His gut tightened at the blow. '*Sì*, I care. We aren't divorced...yet. I don't want other men to get ideas about you.'

'Just be a gentleman and stick to compliments. I spent a small fortune on my dress.'

'Ava, you look breathtaking. That is always a given. But the caveman in me would love to see you in something...else.' A shroud-like *something* that wouldn't make any red-blooded male wonder if her skin felt as soft and velvety as it looked.

She planted a hand on her hip, a pulse-heating smile playing on her glossy lips. 'What exactly is wrong with it?' she challenged, her eyes sparking fire at him.

His frustration escalated. 'Aside from the fact that it barely covers your backside and is missing a back, you mean?' It was just too damn *shimmery*.

'But I look hot?' she pressed with a smile that now dripped pure mischief.

'You look hot. You look like a pure, sinfully tempting fantasy. Is that *gentlemanly* enough for you?' The material caressed her thighs, brought attention to legs that seemed to go on for ever. And she'd done something to her toes. 'What's that?' he rasped, barely able to take a full breath.

She followed his gaze. 'It's a toe ring,' she replied. 'Cesare, we have twenty-five minutes to get there. Will you be able to handle me looking like this or are we going to be late because you've suddenly developed a dislike for any other man seeing me in a short dress?'

He swallowed, tried to speak and ended up just shaking his head as her gaze wandered over him.

'Oh, and for the record, you look hot too. I could tell you to button your shirt all the way up so no woman can see your manly, mouth-watering chest, but see, I'm a grown-up, so I'll just suck it up. Now, shall we go?' Her eyes had grown dark when she raised her gaze to his.

Their expression and the knowledge that she felt an iota of the feelings rampaging through him made him feel marginally better.

'Celine will be made aware in no uncertain terms

that she owes me big for this.' He strolled over to her and held out his arm.

'Behave yourself, Cesare.' At his snarled, pithy response, she laughed. 'This is going to be a long, trying evening, isn't it?'

He took in the thrust of her chin, the hectic race of the pulse in her throat and an all too familiar spike of lust raced to his groin. '*Sì,* it is.'

Cesare knew he was being ridiculous. Jealousy had no place in his feelings because he knew by rights he had no hold on her. Besides, he would bet his sizable fortune that most of the women at the club tonight would be similarly dressed.

But most women weren't his wife!

Another growl emerged before he could stifle it. Cursing the possessiveness that had sprung from nowhere, he grabbed her arm and stalked down the hall. 'I don't begrudge you the dress, *cara.* My only wish is that you'd received *more* of it for your efforts.'

She bared her teeth in a fake smile. 'Well, keep wishing, *tesoro.* Who knows, Santa might come early.'

Ava was only half-listening to the guest whose name she'd forgotten. That he didn't speak more than a dozen words of English made it easy. Her eyes tracked Cesare, who she'd smugly believed hated nightclubs and would hate this evening.

No. Far from smouldering arrogantly the way she remembered him to, he was on the dance floor, enjoying the attentions of the blonde who'd attached herself to him the moment they'd walked in the door.

She glanced down at her dress, and again wondered if she'd been wise to listen to the saleslady at the shop on the Via Condotti who'd insisted the green dress was perfect for her.

Compared to Cesare's dance-partner's dress, Ava's was downright demure. The woman could easily be mistaken for a runway model. Her bone structure alone was enough to make the men here salivate with lust. The fact that she was currently breathing the same air as Cesare didn't seem to deter other men from watching her.

A fist of jealousy lodged in her chest, squeezing until she couldn't breathe.

It didn't help that all day she'd felt on tenterhooks.

She couldn't help but feel her life would unravel even further once she and Cesare finally had their talk.

'You mustn't worry, *il mio amico*. Giuliana is a man-eater, but trust Cesare.'

She turned to find Celine watching her with an expression sickeningly close to pity.

Ava forced out a laugh. 'I'm not worried.'

'I hope it's because you trust him.' Celine's brown eyes narrowed. 'You know he will not deliberately hurt you?'

Anxiety and confusion warred through her. 'Unfortunately, I know nothing of the sort.' Cesare's withdrawal from her had shattered the foundations of her belief.

'Hang in there. Di Goia men don't give their love easily.' Sadness clouded Celine's eyes.

Ava touched her arm. 'Cesare told me about you and Roberto…and Valentina.'

Celine's eyes widened. 'Really?'

She gave a slight grimace. 'I demanded to know his connection to you.'

Celine's smile wobbled. 'I'm glad he told you. Even though *he* loved my sister, Roberto was the love of my life. A part of me is angry he died before I got my chance with him. But it's not too late for you two. Whatever happens, hang on with everything you've got.'

Several minutes after she'd left, Ava remained rooted to the spot, Celine's words echoing through her mind.

She didn't deny Cesare held tremendous sway

over her emotions. One smile was enough to light up her whole day. The occasional glimpses of pain she saw flash through his eyes caused her heart to echo his pain over losing his brother.

But, no matter how she felt about him, she couldn't dismiss the fact that he'd only married her because she'd been pregnant; that he'd tolerated her because she was the mother of his child. Despair rose like a riptide, threatening to suck her down.

The music ended and she watched Cesare and the stunning Giuliana head for the bar. As he plucked two champagne flutes from the counter, his eyes met Ava's. His gaze raked over her, sending her pulse into overdrive.

Suddenly annoyed with his effortless power over her emotions, she lifted her glass in mock salute.

There was no future to hang on to. At least not where she and Cesare were concerned. She didn't doubt his love for Annabelle and therefore didn't doubt his capacity to love. But that love didn't stretch to her.

The distress the thought produced made her glass tremble in her hand.

Setting it down, she found the guest she'd spoken to earlier next to her. Before she could excuse herself, he smiled. Racking her brain, she remem-

bered Celine had introduced him as her second
cousin. He was charmingly good-looking, with
light brown hair and attractively boyish brown
eyes. Not wishing to appear rude, she smiled in
return.

He moved closer. 'Drink?' A champagne-serv-
ing waiter lingered nearby.

Hastily, she shook her head. She'd barely eaten
more than a few mouthfuls at dinner. Drinking on
an empty stomach was a bad idea.

Her admirer set his glass down with a decisive
click.

'Balliamo?' He gestured to the dance floor.
When she hesitated, he clasped a dramatic hand
over his heart. *'Per favore?'*

On a sudden whim, she nodded. She'd never
been one to slink away to lick her wounds. As
much as she wanted to shut herself off, preferably
somewhere quiet, and indulge in a monster ice
cream-fuelled pity party, she wouldn't.

She was here because of Celine. The least she
could do was pretend to enjoy herself.

'Wait.' She laughed when he tried to steer her
towards the dance floor.

His face fell but when he saw her shucking off
her shoes, his grin widened. The blaring hip-hop
was the perfect antidote to her melancholy.

Mario—she remembered his name now—led her to the middle of the dance floor and proceeded to prove himself an energetic dance partner.

The next few songs flew by. Somewhere, during a twirl, her hair clasp slid off and disappeared. Feeling freer, she let go.

When the songs slowed, she stopped dancing, grateful for the chance to cool down. 'Thank you, that was—' She stuttered to a stop when his arms slid around her waist.

Just as quickly she was disengaged from him. She almost lost her balance as rough hands grabbed her from behind. The tingle along her nerve endings announced who held her before she heard his voice.

'It's time to leave.'

Without waiting for her agreement, he tucked her behind him, then murmured low, heated words to Mario. In the strobe light, Ava saw the younger man pale.

Cesare's jaw was set as he straightened and manacled her wrist with one hand.

Before she could draw breath, he was tugging her off the dance floor.

'Cesare, wait!'

He ignored her and headed towards the exit.

'For goodness' sake, stop! I need to get my shoes.'

He stopped so suddenly she careened into him. His hard body easily absorbed the impact, but she was left with a vivid imprint of his broad, bristling masculine form. With his fingers still imprisoning her wrist, his gaze dropped to her feet.

'You danced barefoot?' he grazed out.

'Yes. Now I need to get my shoes.'

'Why? You'll only discard them at the earliest opportunity.'

'That doesn't mean I want to leave them behind. They cost me a bomb.'

His eyes glinted with danger. 'Do *not* move from here.'

The crowd parted for him as he headed for the bar. He returned seconds later, her silver shoes dangling from his fingers. Wordlessly he thrust them at her. When she didn't immediately put them on, his eyebrow shot up.

'What? My feet are killing me.'

His gaze dropped again to her bare feet. For some reason, the sight of them seemed to annoy him further. When he glanced at her, his eyes were ablaze with a look that made her swallow and step back.

He advanced until she was backed into a corner. 'What do you think you were playing at back there?' he asked through clenched teeth.

'I could ask you the same thing.'

He bared his teeth, but nothing about his expression showed he was in a merry mood. 'How long are we going to keep doing this? We've tested the theory a few times these past weeks. *Per favore*, Ava, you need to *stop* pushing my buttons because I'm hanging by a thread here, and I'm seriously scared of what the consequences will mean for us if I snap.'

CHAPTER EIGHT

THE INTENSITY BEHIND his words sent a wave of panic through Ava.

She swallowed, cleared her throat and shook her head. She couldn't show him how his behaviour had affected her. 'You were too busy renewing your various acquaintances to be bothered with me, so I decided to make my own friends.'

Tawny eyes darkened into stormy pools. 'And you thought the best way to enjoy yourself is to let another man put his hands all over you?' His fists were clenched and his pallor had faded a little underneath his tan. The tic beating a wild tattoo in his cheek made her belly swan dive.

'We were just dancing. No big deal.'

His disbelieving laugh grated on her ears. *'No big deal?'*

'What did you expect? That I'd sulk in a corner pining for you?'

He released a harsh breath. 'Ava...'

'You want to leave, so let's go.' Unable to withstand the pressure, she pushed past him and threw open the heavy oak doors that led outside.

The cool breeze after the nightclub's cloying atmosphere was a refreshing welcome. Heaving lungfuls of air into her oxygen-starved body, she stopped beside the bronze and gold column that fronted the club. She sensed Cesare behind her but thought it safer not to turn around.

'We can't keep doing this to one another,' he finally rasped in a fierce undertone.

'I agree. We can't. You've withdrawn from me completely, and yet you can't stand it when another man comes within touching distance of me. Whatever is wrong with us, it's driving me insane and I can't stand this any more.' Feelings she didn't know how to deal with ricocheted through her at lightning speed.

She seethed with anger, she wanted to cry and she wanted to scream.

Plunging shaking hands into her hair, she lifted the suddenly heavy tresses off her heated shoulders. Tears prickled at her eyes but she furiously blinked them away.

Divorce, it seemed, was her only escape. And yet the thought of that final severing from the man she'd dreamed she would spend the rest of her life with brought a hard lump to her chest.

Her frenzied fingers twisted her hair into a rope at her nape.

Cesare drew closer, bringing a renewed rush of awareness. His relentless, all encompassing heat bored down on her. She sucked in a breath and held it in, afraid to let it out lest it somehow transmitted her turmoil.

Firm hands brushed hers away and his strong fingers replaced hers. Her breath grew laboured as his fingers glided through her hair. 'It's time we have that talk, *carissima*.' His breath fanned her sensitive lobe.

A shiver went through her. She'd started to turn when a loud wolf-whistle shattered the air from a trio of men who'd just emerged from the club.

The sight of her—arms raised, bare feet and naked, seductively curved back—garnered very male interest that made Cesare growl low in his throat.

With jerky movements, he shrugged out of his jacket. '*Basta!* I don't care if it offends your female sensibilities. Put this on, *now*,' he hissed. Pulling her arms down, he draped the jacket around her shoulders.

His limo, which had pulled up while she'd been lost in thought, stood with Paolo holding the door open. Cesare ushered her into the back seat, climbed in beside her and yanked the door shut.

Rough fists clenched and unclenched on his thigh, but it wasn't until the car was moving that he spoke.

'It seems you've turned into quite the exhibitionist, *cara mia*.' The cold endearment emerged more as a reproach than an affectionate term.

She flinched and tried to move away. Immediately he trapped her arms, stopping her sideways escape.

'A lot of things have happened while you've been busy pretending I don't exist, Cesare.'

His lips firmed. 'I can see that. And I'm wondering how all this impacts on my daughter.'

She turned sharply. 'Stop right there! You'd better erase that whiff of *you're a bad mother* I hear in your voice, PDQ! And stop referring to her as *your* daughter. Up until very recently, your part in all this has merely been the biology. *You chose to live away from us!* You lost the right to be a father when you withdrew so far physically and emotionally from *our* daughter, she may as well have been dead to you!'

In the darkened interior of the car, his head went back as if she'd struck him. What little colour had remained left his face. She couldn't have struck a deeper blow if she'd shot a bullet into his heart.

Immediately contrite, she reached out and grabbed his hand. It remained cold and unmoving beneath hers.

'Cesare, I didn't mean that—'

'I deserved that. But I had good reason. Or I thought I had for a long time, well before the earthquake. What happened with Roberto and Valentina…I didn't think I deserved a child when Roberto had lost his.'

'Do you really think Roberto begrudged you a family?'

'I didn't think—I knew. He told me many times that I didn't deserve a family—' a tight edge of pain roughened his voice '—that I deserved to be alone the way he was.'

Her insides fractured at his torment. But she couldn't stop her own pain from welling up alongside it. She sank deeper into the warm jacket that had so recently draped Cesare's body. Curiously, she drew strength from it to fight him. 'I'm sorry he said that to you. But did you really think Annabelle deserved to suffer because your brother was fighting his own monsters?'

'It was my duty to protect him—'

'You also had a duty to your wife and child. I know you married me because I was pregnant,' she forced out painfully, 'but you shouldn't have left me alone to bring up our daughter alone.'

A small, taut silence reigned before, 'You were never alone,' he said, almost under his breath. 'You had nannies, household staff and a security detail.'

Rage smashed her burgeoning hope to smithereens. '*Security detail*? Oh, that's all right then. You know I've never been part of a family. I told you how my father and brothers treated me. God, Cesare, I had no idea what I was doing when I had a baby. I expected you to stick around and help me, be with me. Instead you jumped on your jet at the first opportunity, and chased deal after deal. I didn't marry your household staff or your security detail. I married you! *You* should have been there, not them!'

His hand tightened painfully on hers and his head dipped in solemn acknowledgement. 'I should've been. No matter my inadequacies as a husband, I should've tried harder as a father. Trust me, Ava, I know my failings where my daughter is concerned.' He spread his fingers in a purely Latin gesture. 'It's why I'm here now, trying to right that wrong. I intend not to lose sight of the fact that she is the most important thing in all of this.'

Hearing the words—so resolute and promising where their daughter was concerned, and so excluding where she was—made Ava's heart catch so painfully she couldn't speak for several seconds. But she didn't need to. Cesare was in the mood to unburden himself. '*Dio mio*, Ava, you must remember we barely knew each other before you got pregnant and yet you so quickly put me front and centre of everything you wanted in a family. I couldn't think straight. You say you had no idea what you were doing but to me you seemed the epitome of calm and composure. When, after a while, you didn't seem to need me, I left.'

Ava reeled, fiercely glad she wasn't standing up, for surely she'd have lost the power of her legs. Her spine turned liquid and she collapsed into the soft leather seat. 'I had no idea...'

The rest of her words dried up as he shook his head, raised a silencing hand before clenching it into a fist mid-air. The action, so wrought with despair, made her inhale sharply. She glanced at his profile.

The corresponding look of wrenching pain on his face made her reach out.

'Cesare—'

* * *

Cesare couldn't stop the hiss of pain that slipped through his lips. 'Enough! Do not say another word.'

Regret, self-condemnation, jealousy and anger all coalesced into a seething ball of emotion in his chest. Emotions he'd been fighting what felt like forever sank their steely talons deeper into him. He was exhausted... *Dio, was* he exhausted.

'I'm tired of trading verbal blows with you, Ava.'

He needed a distraction, and he reached for the only thing that had ever been potent enough to melt his control.

Ava's gasp echoed in the car as he yanked her against him.

Soft contours moulded against his hardness, her eyes widening as she encountered a particularly stiff part of him. His gaze dropped to her lips, his focus hazing at the thought of possessing her, of washing away the tide of blackness that threatened to consume him in the most effective way he knew how.

He slanted his lips over hers, and nearly groaned. Heady, seductive, infinitely dangerous to him. But, right at that moment, he didn't care about the danger. He wanted a reprieve from the demons clamouring for his soul.

With a feathery sigh, she melted into him and

he exhaled in satisfaction. He'd expected bristle and bite, for her to fight the way she always did. Instead she sank further into him.

His tongue, eager to taste, captured hers. Another gasp echoed in the silent interior as his fingers explored what he'd been itching to explore for far too long.

No woman had ever tasted like Ava. Innocent and bewitching, bold and insecure—one minute she kissed him as if she wanted to devour him, the next she whimpered with a touch of timidity.

The heady mix made him harder, torturing him with the need to pull up the short hemline that had been taunting him all evening and just *take, take, take.*

But, as much as he wanted to rip her panties off, spread her open on the wide limo seat and pleasure them both until one of them passed out, he couldn't.

There's nothing wrong with kissing, his insistent body clamoured. He deepened the kiss, letting his mouth perform the task his body couldn't be allowed to. Ava's mouth opened wider, her tongue growing bolder in its own exploration.

A dark thought seeped into his mind. Fighting the blackness, he wrenched his lips from hers.

'You never answered me when I asked if there'd been anyone else. I need to know.'

'Why, so you can go growl at them the way you did with Mario tonight?'

Irrational jealousy he'd experienced earlier returned. He planted a hard kiss on her lips, determined to wipe the feeling away with the smooth sweep of his tongue.

'Mario has been left in no doubt as to the consequences should he ever dare to come within three feet of you again.' He hesitated a beat. 'Ava?'

Mesmerising green eyes held his. 'I'm still a married woman. I take my vows very seriously.' She sniffed, and her eyes darkened. 'Has there been for you?'

He shook his head. 'We're still married, *mia amante*. I would never dishonour you in that way.'

Her eyes darkened and her swollen lower lip trembled. 'How can you say things like that to me and expect me not to have hope for us?'

His insides clenched. 'Ava…'

'For God's sake, shut up, Cesare. Just…shut up and kiss me.'

He didn't need to be told twice.

Lust thundering forcefully through him, he went deeper. She was all fire now, voracious and demanding, her hands frantic as they grasped his nape, grabbed his hair and twisted it between her fingers. His heart tore around his chest like a crazed animal. When her full breasts pressed against his chest, he nearly lost his mind.

His hand moved to her back, encountered sleek, smooth flesh. He pulled back, sucked in a deep breath and watched her fight for breath too. The sight of her moistened, kiss-swollen lips made him groan.

'What?' she asked huskily. Her fingers still worked through his hair, scraped his scalp. He'd never have imagined such a simple gesture could be erotic, but the fierce throb of his erection indicated otherwise.

'We've arrived at the apartment.'

It took a few seconds for his words to register. In that suspended time, he basked in her warm supple body plastered against him.

Eyes widening, she sprang away from him. The loss was a fist in his gut. She reached for his jacket and settled it around her shoulders and, oddly, Cesare felt comforted that she had a part of him on her. He toyed with asking Paolo to take them on a long drive out of the city but already the door was opening.

She stepped out, exhibiting an obscene amount

of leg, and her bare feet made him want to growl some more.

He carried her shoes and trailed her into the building. He'd chosen to lead a separate life away from his wife and child because he hadn't thought he had what it took to be a husband and father. He'd drifted through each day, doing what needed to be done—making deals, making more money, taking financial care of his parents.

Now he was hyperaware of every passing minute, of every atom of his being poised on a knife-edge of sharp focus. Focus on the woman in front of him, her stunning body and shapely backside swaying underneath his jacket as she strode towards the lift on the balls of her bare feet.

Inside the lift, he caught her to him but didn't kiss her. If he started he wouldn't be able to stop.

Once they were inside the apartment, he kicked the door shut with his foot and reached for her. What he grabbed instead was his jacket, held out by Ava with a determined look on her face.

'Come here,' he commanded, every muscle tight with need.

She raised her chin, exposing the satin neck that sent his pulse sky-high. 'No.'

Shock froze him in place. *'Che?'*

She remained defiant and out of reach. 'I won't

sleep with you just because you've decided that you want me again.'

He prowled towards her. She backed away, making him want to pounce on her. He cautioned himself not to. 'Again? Hell, haven't we proved conclusively that I've never stopped wanting you? *Dio*, you only have to walk into a room to make me rock-hard for you.'

Heat bloomed in her cheeks, appeasing him somewhat. As did her soft lips parting on a breath. The fierce shake of her head, however, plunged him back towards supreme frustration. Again he tried to reach for her. Again she danced out of his reach. Irritation sizzled through him.

'As hot as that was intended to make me—'

'Did I succeed?'

The rapid rise and fall of her breasts gave him his answer. 'I'm not going to fall into bed with you, Cesare.'

She shook out his jacket like a matador trying to distract a raging bull. He ignored it and focused on his prize. Another step brought him closer to her. He breathed in her scent and acknowledged that his need for her was beyond his own understanding.

And he was infinitely weary of twisting himself into knots about it.

'Tell me you don't want me, *mia sposa*.'

'You know I do, but I won't let you toy with me. What happened to—*this is as far as you're ever going to get?*'

Unwelcome heat crawled up his neck. For a man who had a superb command of words, he couldn't compose a suitable answer aside from the pure, unadulterated truth. 'We both know that bikini should've come with a skull and crossbones warning. I was angry with you for killing me with temptation and wasn't quite myself when I uttered those words.' Having Ava taunt him with her body when he'd been fighting his desire had been the last straw. He hadn't liked being held on the knife-edge of control, as he'd been right from the beginning with her.

'And now you've just decided *to hell with it*?'

Stalking away from her, he tore off his constricting tie and tossed it away. 'I haven't decided anything! What I do know is that you're driving me crazy and...' His fist clenched. 'Dammit, Ava, you flaunted yourself so blatantly.'

'Well, you're in luck. I'm not flaunting anything any more. Goodnight, Cesare.'

At first he couldn't comprehend what was happening. By the time the shock wore off, Ava's deliciously tempting back had disappeared down the hall and into the guest bedroom.

Unclenching his fist, he raked his decidedly unsteady fingers through his hair. *Bravo, Cesare.* He'd finally succeeded at what he'd been trying to do since Ava returned—he'd pushed her away.

Except satisfaction tasted like ashes and thwarted lust sucked. He swore and paced the room. It was no use asking himself what he'd been thinking.

When it came to Ava, she only had to touch him and he lost his mind. She only had to look at him with those smoky emerald eyes and his senses flamed with the promise of pleasure.

He spotted his briefcase and his jaw tightened. He strode to it and pulled out the papers. The cold, stark words taunted him. With a simple stroke of his name along the dotted line, he could be free of this madness.

But was that his only option?

Ava's words in the car struck him. From the beginning, he'd known she had a strained relationship with her own family. To all intents and purposes, he and Annabelle were the only family she had. He'd married her, only to leave her to her own devices because he'd been too caught up in his own angst to see clearly.

Was he man enough to start now?

His fist tightened around the papers. On a decisive thought, he ripped them in two. He'd been too long locked in his own pain for his part in Roberto's seclusion, he hadn't stopped to think about Ava's needs when she married him.

A grim smile crossed his mouth. Had Ava asked for a divorce two months ago, hell, even the day before the earthquake, he probably would have granted it. But not now. He ripped the papers until they were indecipherable pieces.

He still didn't have it in him to offer her what she wanted, but he, if nothing else, was a damned good negotiator. There would be no divorce.

So what now?

Hell if he knew. He would just have to work it out later.

CHAPTER NINE

AVA PACED THE length of the guest room, unable to calm her frenzied pulse or her mind's racing.

First Cesare pushed her away, then he wanted her to fall into his arms. She squeezed her eyes shut and tried to quell her body's clamouring for what she'd stubbornly denied it. But her pulse wouldn't quieten. The thought that she'd come within a hair's breadth of making love to Cesare again after so long sent her pacing faster. She should be thankful she'd resisted him.

Yeah, right.

Truth was, she wanted to jump her husband so badly, she could barely think straight. The heat of his body, the intoxicating scent of his hard-packed muscles rose in her mind like the promise of a delectable feast after an endless famine.

Would that be so wrong?

She felt herself sway towards the door and dug her toes hard into the luxurious carpet. What was she thinking? Sure, he'd been shocked when she walked away from him. *But he hadn't followed. And he's not exactly breaking down your door, is he?*

While she was in here torturing herself, he was probably enjoying the view, nightcap in hand, or halfway to securing another multi-million euro deal.

Whirling, she stalked to the window.

The stunning vista of night time Rome lay before her. Cesare's penthouse apartment sat atop a converted luxury villa off *Campo de Fiori* and commanded views as far as the Vatican and St Peter's Dome.

Was he staring at the same view? Raising a hand to the window, she watched her skin heat the cool glass. The view outside faded when she caught a glimpse of herself in the reflection.

Wild, fiery hair, tangled into shameless disarray by Cesare's seeking hands. Her eyes were wide pools of confusion and hurt she wanted to hide away from and her lips were swollen and bruised with Cesare's kisses. She wasn't surprised to see her chest rise and fall as if she'd run a marathon.

And all because of the man whose presence impacted her life and emotions as effortlessly as if she were a puppet on his string.

Her breath rushed out, frosted the glass, distorting her view as she remembered… In the fevered chaos of the kiss and the argument that had followed, they'd never got round to talking about the solution to their problems.

She eyed the door, then almost in a trance, her hand went to the button securing her dress at her nape. With one short fumble, it pooled at her feet. She contemplated taking a shower, but feared her resolve would desert her if she delayed for too long.

Padding to the dresser, she picked up her hairbrush. The rhythmic strokes reinforced her strength, which in turn abated the haunted look in her eyes. She hadn't needed a bra with her dress, but she still wore her thong. The thought of going to Cesare naked heated up her blood, but she quickly abandoned the idea.

Crossing to the wardrobe, she selected a short forest-green silk night slip and matching gown of hers she'd found when she'd unpacked earlier. Shrugging them on, she tied the gown and quickly left the room before she lost her nerve.

The hallway was as quiet as when she'd walked down it a short while ago. The dimmed light in the living room revealed it as empty as the kitchen and terrace.

The idea of confronting Cesare in his bedroom sent a confidence-shaking shiver of alarm through her. Slowly, she walked towards his door and paused outside. Catching her lower lip between her teeth, she listened for sound within. What if he was asleep?

Or, worse, he'd reverted to the cool, distant man she'd grown to hate this past year? Fear of rejection dried her mouth but she didn't back down. Inhaling deeply, she turned the knob.

He was lounging against the king-size bed's intricately designed headboard, a glass of cognac in one hand and an electronic tablet in the other.

His gaze snapped and locked on hers. Slowly he placed the glass on the nightstand.

Ava's eyes landed on his bare chest and hot air seared her lungs. She'd seen his naked torso many times but the sheer magnitude of his potent masculinity never ceased to raise her temperature.

'To what do I owe the pleasure, *cara*?'

Her tongue darted out to moisten dry lips. 'Our talk...I want to have it...now.'

He turned away from her, shielding his expression from her as he laid the tablet down. 'Are you sure that's what you come for? To *talk?*' His eyes narrowed and he linked his hands together over his hard, ridged stomach. Despite his stance, he reminded her of a hunt-mode predator, ready to pounce with merciless precision.

Her fingers clenched on the doorknob. 'Yes.'

He nodded, grabbed the corner of the sheet and drew it back. 'Then, by all means, make yourself comfortable and let's…talk.'

She didn't need to look to know he was naked. Cesare slept in the nude. 'Are you…are you going to put any clothes on?'

'No.'

'Cesare…'

'I don't know what that would achieve. I told you what happens to me when you enter my presence. Clothed or *in flagrante*, the effect is the same.'

Desire punched a hole in her belly. Dangerous, treacherous desire. She needed to leave, only she couldn't move. 'But…'

He sighed. 'I don't want to have this talk with you all the way across the room, Ava. Come here, it's much more comfortable, I promise,' he murmured silkily.

She shook her head and pulled the door open, her bravado deserting her. 'You know what? Maybe this wasn't a great idea. It's way past midnight and…I can't deal with you this way. We…we both need to get some sleep. We'll talk in the morn—'

Quicker than she'd ever imagined it possible for him to move, he sprang off the bed, shot across the room and slammed his hand against the door.

Her gasp was strangled in her throat as he pressed his hot, bristling *naked* length against her back.

'Oh no, Ava *mia*. You do not get to flounce off for a second time,' he breathed hotly in her ear.

'I don't *flounce!*'

'No. You sway. You mesmerise. You capture and hold my attention until I feel like I'm drowning in your seductive beauty.'

'I don't know what on earth you're talking about…'

'Oh *sì,* you do. Or you wouldn't be here now. I'll give you what you want, *tesoro mio.* We will have that talk. But there's a very high possibility that you'll hate me when we do.'

She gasped and turned within the circle of his arms. 'Why would I hate you? You said there'd been no one else!' A sickening feeling invaded her at the thought that he'd lied about that.

His eyes burned into hers. 'I meant it.'

Relief poured through her. 'Then what else could there possibly be? Unless you're about to confess you're some psycho serial killer?'

Her comment didn't lighten the mood as she'd expected. Instead his jaw tightened, then released. 'I did have homicidal thoughts about Mario to-night. In fact, I had unholy thoughts about every man at the party who dared to look at you.'

'I'm surprised you had a chance to notice, seeing how you were so enamoured of Giuliana's bosom.'

He shifted even closer until his granite-hard arousal pressed against her pelvis. He gave a low, deep laugh. 'It seems we've both been clawed by the sharp talons of the green-eyed monster.'

Pain stabbed through her desire. 'Jealousy would imply that we care for each other, Cesare.'

His smile slowly faded, replaced by a growing hunger as his gaze slowly raked her face as if imprinting it on his brain. '*Sì,* it would. I never denied that I care about you, Ava.'

'But only sexually?'

'Don't underestimate the power of sex, *mia cara.* It has brought down kingdoms and ruined powerful men.' As if to emphasise its power, he leaned into her.

'So far you've managed to remain untouched by it,' she croaked.

His thick arousal registered boldly against her belly at the same time as his mouth settled heavily over hers.

The power of thought instantly deserted her. This kiss was nothing like they'd shared in the car. This was a full, unapologetic assault on her senses, a bold display of Cesare's power and the firm intent of what he meant to happen between them. His tongue stroked boldly against hers, performing a dangerous dance that had only one destination.

Heat swelled and rocketed straight to her core. The shock of how quickly her body reacted to him made her head spin, but even that reaction was ruthlessly swept aside under the torrent of need building inside her.

Her fingers encountered Cesare's naked torso. Her nails bit deep and she revelled in the groan that shuddered through him.

He raised his head, his breathing harsh in the darkened room. With a quick dip, he licked her tingling lips. 'I'm far from untouched, *cara*. Hasn't it always been this way between us?' he demanded thickly. 'One touch and the whole world burns up?' As if to demonstrate, he ran a lazy finger down the side of her neck.

'Yes.' Her moan brought a satisfied smile to his face.

Bringing his hands onto her shoulders, he eased the robe from her. The gown followed, but she barely felt it slither off her arms to fall to the floor, entranced as she was by the molten heat in his eyes.

With unsteady fingers, he traced a path from her neck, down between her breasts to her belly until he grazed the top of her thong.

Words, murmured in Italian appreciation, tumbled from his lips.

'English, please. I need to understand what you're saying.'

He repeated the raw, explicit words. When her face flamed, he laughed and reverted to Italian. Every syllable touched her skin like a kiss, making her limbs lust-heavy until all she could do was sag against the door as his touch drummed a beat of desire through her.

'Cesare,' she sighed, unable to form a more coherent sentence past the sweet benediction of his name on her lips. Gathering every last ounce of strength, she pulled back. 'We…we still need to talk.'

He dropped another hungry kiss at the corner of her mouth. 'We will. But I need…we both need this before we do. And, whatever happens, Ava, please know this now. I'm very sorry I hurt you.'

Tears gathered in her eyes and clogged her throat. When they spilled onto her cheeks, he wiped them away with his thumbs.

With a sigh, he scooped her in his arms and carried her to the bed.

Sheets warmed by his body immediately engulfed her in his scent. When he stepped back and she saw, really saw him—naked, magnificent and needy—desire dragged through her belly, amplifying the power of her own need, propelling her to reach for him, to make sure he was real and not a figment of her fevered imagination.

'Come closer.'

He complied. She reached up and traced the sculpted lines of his face, from hollowed cheek, over smooth lips to the rough shadow of his stubble. When she made another pass over his lips, he snagged her fingers in his teeth. Boldly, he sucked on her forefinger.

Fresh fires of desire licked through her. Her nipples, long puckered into nubs of excruciating need, hardened further. Without releasing her fingers, Cesare settled down beside her and placed one hand below her breast. Her temperature shot up another notch.

'Touch me, please,' she pleaded. But he just rested his hand there, under the curve of her breast, while he leisurely sucked on her finger.

Liquid heat oozed between her thighs. Her lids grew heavy as the motion of his mouth tugged her closer to the edge of ecstasy.

His hand edged closer to her breast.

Moaning with desperation, she tried to move closer to his touch. With a final, hot lick he released her finger. His gaze blazed down at her, dissecting her every reaction. 'Not yet.'

Pressure built in her nipples, almost as painful as the relentless heat pulsing between her legs. Just when she thought she couldn't stand the pressure any longer, his hand traced the underside of her breast. She jerked in protest and moaned as he started to perform slow, excruciating circles on her flesh. With every rotation bringing him close but not close enough to the aching pinnacle, Ava feared she would die from need.

Finally, at the point of begging, he slanted his mouth over hers, and closed his thumb and forefinger over her nipple.

Her cry was swallowed up into his mouth. Her orgasm slammed into her with the force of a tornado, twisting and tossing her high, leaving her no room to breathe.

Firelight exploded behind her lids as ecstasy awakened and tore through her. Through it all, Cesare kept his mouth on hers, lapping up her cries of bliss.

The intensity of his kiss lessened as she slowly floated back to earth. When she could bring herself to open her eyes, he was gazing down at her, his eyes full of heat and something close to wonder.

'You're still so responsive, *tesoro mio,*' he rasped.

'I thought my fevered imagination had conjured it up in the hallway two weeks ago, but I know different now. You've never lost it.'

'Does that please you?' she asked in a husky voice.

'That sex between us has always been raw and intensely special? I'm a red-blooded Latin man, am I not?' came the smug response.

Her fingers closed over his rock-hard bicep, renewed need clawing through her. 'Maybe you should demonstrate, before I die of anticipation?'

A curious expression flitted over his face, gone quickly before she could decipher it. She started to ask him what was wrong, but lost her train of thought when he chose that moment to kiss her again.

By the time he raised his head to rasp, 'Are you still on the Pill?' she could barely string coherent words together to answer.

'Yes,' she croaked.

He recaptured her mouth, then rolled them over so she was on top of him. The first touch of his bare chest against her breasts sent her fevered pulse rocketing once more. Unable to resist, she rubbed herself against him. His deep groan only fed her hunger.

* * *

Against her thigh, Cesare's erection pulsed, hot and insistent. She rolled her hips against him, the friction driving her quickly to distraction. His hands clasped her bottom, impatient fingers diving beneath the elastic to brand her flesh.

Another moan filled the room, her heart's frenzied beats echoing in her ears until she could hear nothing but the promise of bliss, feel nothing but the equally intoxicating pounding of Cesare's heart.

One hand fisted in her hair and drew her back. Tawny heat-filled eyes caressed her face. *'Perdono, cara,* but I have to do this.'

Before she could ask what he meant, the sound of tearing fabric ripped through the room. 'God, that is so macho,' she teased on a pant.

He grinned. 'I don't have time to ease it from your hips.'

'What do you have time for?'

'This,' he whispered, raised his head and rolled his tongue over one nipple before sucking it into his mouth.

Her cry was loud, desperate and tinged with pain as pleasure arrowed forcefully through her. Her back arched under the intensity of her delight. Cesare suckled harder, then relented to lick her burning flesh. Before she could draw breath, he repeated the action. Her fingers convulsed in his hair as pleasure consumed her.

Once again bliss beckoned and she rushed blindly towards it. But, just as she was about to dive into the abyss, he pulled back.

With a quick motion, he flipped her underneath him and knelt between her thighs. He pulled open a drawer and extracted a condom.

Watching him rip open the contraception sent a bold thought through her head. Rising to face him, she placed her hands on his. 'Let me.'

Cesare's eyes widened. 'You've never done that before.'

'I've had a long time to think about us, like this. Will you let me?'

He nodded and handed it over. That her offer pleased him and intensified the fire of arousal in his eyes only spurred her on.

She crawled on the bed until she was behind him. With an open-mouthed kiss between his shoulder blades that sent a fevered shudder through him, she took over the task. The powerful breadth of his shoulders meant she couldn't see what she was doing, but her touch was enough.

Slowly, glorying in his potent, silky arousal, she slid the condom over his erection. Smooth, velvety skin veined with his thick blood surged underneath her fingers.

She bit the flesh she'd kissed moments before and felt her own fever rise as he trembled.

'*Tesoro,* I fear your disappointment if you don't cease this torture.' His voice was pained, tinged with a desperation that matched her own.

Equally desperate for him, she completed her task quickly, but couldn't resist a last caress of his hard flesh.

'*Per favore,* I need you,' he pleaded hoarsely.

Twisting around, he grabbed her and returned her to her original position.

Sure hands grasped her thighs and spread them wide. Her scent rose between them like a potent aphrodisiac. Cesare's gaze dropped to her open sex and his eyes darkened to a burnished bronze.

Swallowing hard, he murmured, 'I had forgotten how exquisitely beautiful you are down there.'

Sweet pleasure stole through her. Reaching up, she curled her hand into his smooth, hard chest. 'I never forgot, for a single moment, how beautiful *you* are.'

To her he would always be a god among men, the powerful, captivating figure who had gripped her attention from the moment they'd met and had never let go, despite everything that had happened between them since.

He glided his fingers down her inner thighs, trailing a path of fire that threatened to ignite her very core. She bit her lip, fighting the haze that encroached, the promise of heaven suspended just out of reach. But this time she wanted more, wanted the power of Cesare deep inside her to be the only thing that triggered her ecstasy.

Which was why she wasn't prepared for the skilled finger that slid inside her sensitive opening.

Her spine arched clear off the bed. 'Cesare!' His name was a cry ripped from her throat, a cry that sounded again when his thumb swiftly found her nub of desire. Blood pounded through her veins, crashed through her head until it was the only thing she could hear.

He groaned as her fingers bit into his shoulders. Her head thrashed against the pillows, fighting but knowing she was losing the headlong flight into rapture. The brief reprieve she experienced when he gently removed his fingers was easily lost again when the blunt head of his powerful erection replaced his fingers.

'Open your eyes, Ava.'

Weakly, she obeyed.

Curling her legs around his hips, he plucked her

hands from his shoulders and placed them both above her head. 'Now don't move.'

His gaze stayed on hers as he rocked forward. At the first thrust, every instinct urged her hips to move. 'I can't not…it's too much…'

'You can. Just do it.' He fed more of himself into her, stretching unused muscles and sending her senses into near freefall. Her heart hammered, her lungs begged for air and the sheer pressure of being filled by Cesare threatened her sanity.

Finally, he was deep inside her. His gaze fixed on hers, he held still, allowing her to savour the full force of his possession. Time suspended between them, the only sound their shared breath as the power of being joined held them in thrall.

At last, he breathed, 'Now.'

They moved at the same time, slamming together with a force that rocked worlds. His grunt of pleasure triggered her shuddering moan. Pleasure like she'd never known surged through her. Clamping her legs tighter around him, she met him thrust for thrust, falling into a long-forgotten rhythm like a song to a lark. The world fell away.

Nothing else mattered but Cesare, his sounds of ecstasy filled her ears as he thrust over and over inside her.

Her flesh welcomed him, enclosing him in a

tight, silken embrace that gradually milked his pleasure. His face contorted in a mask of pained pleasure as he crept closer to the edge.

In the single moment before all became lost, Ava glimpsed a connection, an unspoken bond that drew at her heartstrings and made her catch her breath. Before she could analyse it, she was swept away. Holding back was not an option so she flew towards ecstasy and a release that annihilated every single thought. Unable to bear the assault, she clamped her eyes shut. Firelight rained again, showering her in pleasure so profound, tears prickled the back of her lids.

Above her, triggered by her relentless convulsions, Cesare hurtled towards his own release. For a split second, he stilled, his whole being gripped tight in indescribable sensation. Her legs around his back strained to keep him locked against her. With a final desperate groan, he gave up control, managing just in time to adjust his position before he collapsed on top of her.

Ava drew her arms around him, her fingers slowly caressing his sweat-slicked flesh as shudders chased through him. Somewhere in the lost minutes, he turned his head and planted kisses along her jaw, but no words were uttered. None were needed.

She couldn't recall when he finally disengaged from her but she had a vague sense of being settled against him. But something different tripped her senses. It wasn't until she was drifting off to sleep, his strong arms coming around to anchor her to him and soft words gently ushering her into sleep, that she realised what it was.

In the moments before his climax, Cesare had pulled out of her.

CHAPTER TEN

CESARE STOOD AT the foot of the bed, gazing down at his sleeping wife. Guilt bit hard into him. Although a careful inspection of the condom had set his mind at ease somewhat, he didn't delude himself into thinking that would be the case every time.

Their passion hadn't abated in their time apart. If anything, the opposite was true. He'd had to stop himself from taking her in the raw and earthy way his senses had clamoured for him to, and he didn't fool himself into believing he would always remain in control. Ava needed only to be within touching distance to erode his willpower.

His senses sprang to life again as she shifted and stretched on the bed, baring a little more of her body.

He locked his knees to stop himself from crawling back beside her. When his feet disobeyed, he clung to the bedpost, gritting his teeth as arousal fired deep inside. For a split second he resented the unrelenting need Ava had always elicited in him.

From the first moment he'd laid eyes on her at that busy intersection in London, something vital had shifted inside him, knocked him sideways. He'd labelled it as lust back then, but now he wasn't so sure it was mere lust. Lust faded. But the thought of Ava walking out of his life permanently made his chest tighten in fierce rejection.

She murmured in her sleep. Every sinew in his body protested at the idea but he forced himself to take a step towards the door.

'Cesare?' Her soft voice stopped him in his tracks.

She was sitting up, the sheets slipping to her waist. Her lush curves gleamed in the ambient light. Her nipples, half hidden by the heavy fall of her fiery hair, crested breasts he longed to mould and caress again. His body's instant reaction made him swallow hard. It was that or risk choking. He hadn't had sex in a year. His need was more than great, but staying would mean pushing his luck way above acceptable levels.

'What are you doing out of bed?' she asked.

'Letting you get some sleep, *amante.*'

Slowly she sagged back against the pillows. Her hair parted, revealing the full allure of her breasts.

In a slow, seductive sweep designed to drive him insane, her gaze left his and caressed its way down his nude body.

His heart hammered as she boldly stared at his erection. When she moistened her lips, a rough tremor coursed through him.

'I'm wide awake now,' she stated in a husky murmur.

Heat rushed through him, propelling him forward before he could form a single thought. When he reached the side of the bed, he paused. 'I don't want to make you sore.' She'd been tight when they'd made love. There'd been no one else. The thought sent a powerful surge of primitive possession through him. If he got his way, and he would once he dedicated enough strategic thinking to the issue, his wife would know no other man but him.

'It wasn't that bad.'

Unable to help himself, he traced his finger along the warm colour that crept up her neck into her cheeks. 'Are we rating my performance or your soreness? My delicate ego seeks clarification.'

Her gaze dropped to his engorged male flesh, one brow raised as her sinful mouth curved. 'There's nothing delicate about you, *caro.*'

His breath fractured. Somewhere inside it registered that this was the first genuine smile he'd witnessed from her in a long time.

The thought that he'd missed it without realising his loss hit him squarely in the chest. Before he could assess his actions, he lifted the sheet and slid in next to her.

'On the contrary, I'm as delicate as a baby when you look at me like that.'

'Like what?'

'Like I'm the sole focus of your world.'

Her smile slowly faded. 'You were my only focus, Cesare. For a very long time. Then you took yourself away.' Her voice caught and his heart caught with it.

Leaning down, he kissed her, his chest tightening with the need to offer reassurance he had no right to give.

'I'm here now,' he offered instead.

It was inadequate, and her darkening eyes told him so. But he had no solution. Not yet. So he did the next best thing. He deepened the kiss, infusing her with his crazy desire for her, savouring her immediate and complete response. Pleasure, hot and fervid, rose inside when her hands moved around his back and held him tight.

Ava's thigh slid between his, creating mind-altering sensations that washed away his troubled thoughts.

When her hand closed over him, a groan erupted from his very soul. Feeling himself slide closer to the edge, he quickly reached for another condom.

'Not yet,' she rasped in between planting hot open-mouthed kisses on his chest. With a firm hand, she propelled him onto his back and rose onto her knees. Her nails scraped along his torso. His dark curse brought another smile.

'You're enjoying your power?'

'I'm enjoying…something.' Her eyes danced with delight, then she leaned down and boldly tongued his nipple.

His heartfelt groan earned him another flick of her tongue. He clenched his fingers in her silky Titian hair, holding her close as he lost himself in the pleasure that filled his every cell. With every breath, every inch lower she went, he skated closer to the edge of madness. She sank her teeth into the skin below his navel and his heart stopped.

'Ava…' He wasn't sure whether he warned or pleaded.

In response, she closed both hands on him, caressed him up and down.

'*Dio mio*. Again.' A definite plea this time.

She complied, her gaze rising to snag his as she

moved her firm grip over him. She maintained eye contact as she caressed him, a boldness in her actions he'd never witnessed before. The look, coupled with the mind-bending effect of her hands, scattered his thoughts. She leaned in closer, parted her lips and took him in her mouth and it was in that moment Cesare knew the true meaning of insanity.

He barely remembered passing her the condom when she demanded it. He was so consumed with her, he couldn't see straight. He welcomed her when she positioned herself over him, her beautiful body poised to take him inside her heat.

Her gasp of pleasure triggered his own, and just like before they found their own unique rhythm, the sheer bliss of their coming together so mind-blowing he was at the point of no return before he knew it.

Cesare forced himself to hang on despite the teeth-grinding need to let go. The effort it took was monumental, especially in the moment when Ava slammed down onto him one final time before losing herself in her blistering orgasm.

'Oh God,' she rasped as she collapsed onto him, her spasms causing him to see stars as he waited… waited… 'God, Cesare, I've missed you so much.'

The heartbreak in her voice made his gut tighten painfully.

'I've missed you too,' he responded gruffly. Her spasms gentled. He gripped her hips and pushed his hard length inside her, finally permitting himself to take his own pleasure. It didn't take long. With one final thrust, he pulled out of her. Ava jerked in surprise. He kissed her and she melted into him. He groaned in pleasure, unwilling to entertain the tinge of regret permeating his pleasure as he lost himself in his climax.

Several minutes later, their breaths calmed. Against his chest, Ava murmured sleepily. As he caressed his fingers through her hair, Cesare knew without a shadow of a doubt that he would fight Fate herself for a solution if he had to.

Ava walked into the large sunlit kitchen and immediately saw the note pinned to the fridge door. She'd woken to an empty bed, an empty apartment and troubled thoughts.

Her intention last night had been to find a definitive solution to the state of her marriage. Instead she'd fallen under her husband's spell. Again. Pulling her robe around her, she padded further into the kitchen. Plucking the note from the magnet, she read Cesare's sprawled, bold writing.

Gone to get breakfast. Present for you on cof-fee table. C.

She studied the complicated-looking coffee ma-chine for several minutes before pressing the least harmful-looking button. Crossing her fingers that it wouldn't end in disaster, she trod on cool wooden floors to the all-white, stunningly decorated liv-ing room that boasted floor-to-ceiling windows.

Her heart skipped a beat as she eyed the large, exquisitely packaged box. Raising the lid, she gasped at its contents.

The camera was one she'd coveted for a long time but had never thought she'd own because of its astronomical price. State-of-the-art, with a zoom lens and sharpness beyond anything she'd ever seen, it was the crème-de-la-crème of cam-eras.

Her fingers tingled as she lifted its heavy but comfortable weight. It had already been assem-bled and a gleeful smile curved her lips when she turned it on.

Rushing out onto the terrace, she focused and snapped a series of panoramic pictures, making sure to catch the iconic St Peter's Dome in the frame. She took a few closer still—Campo de Fiori a few hundred metres away, the ever-present fountains that could be found all over the city, and the awe-inspiring statues that Rome was famous for.

Leaning over, she focused her camera on the street below. Several residents enjoyed breakfast at outside cafés that shot off from the square. She zoomed in with her finger poised to click, only to pause when a familiar figure swung into view.

Ava lowered the camera and stared.

In the morning sunlight, the sight of Cesare in a torso-hugging T-shirt and jeans stole her breath. He held a container bearing her favourite breakfast *trattoria*'s logo in one hand, a newspaper tucked under his arm and his phone to his ear. A slight breeze ruffled his hair, and several women seated outside a smart café turned to ogle his long-legged body as he passed.

He seemed oblivious to the looks. In fact he seemed far away. Slowly, she lifted the camera and zoomed in on the man she'd shared her body with last night.

She clicked several times, the professional in her adjusting the camera to make the most of every single frame. But with each picture she took, her heart lurched.

Without warning, he stopped. The newspaper fell from his arm and Ava saw his face whiten. For several minutes he stared into space, until a scooter backfired in the distance, galvanising him into motion, the newspaper discarded.

When he disappeared from view to enter the apartment building, Ava slowly lowered the camera. With dread, she glanced down at the pictures she'd captured.

Ice clutched her heart as she reviewed each frame. Far from looking like a man who'd just left his wife's bed sated and happy, Cesare looked as if he was caught in the middle of a living nightmare.

The sun disappeared behind a cloud, momentarily casting the terrace in shadow. The portentous effect wasn't lost on her.

She'd risked her heart again by sleeping with Cesare last night. A heart that had never completely healed from being battered once. Now she knew she'd placed it in harm's way again.

Her fingers clenched around the camera when she heard Cesare's key in the lock. Taking a deep breath, she walked into the living room just as he entered.

He saw her and paused. Wordlessly, his gaze raked over her, sending her pulse on a roller coaster dive.

'Thank you for this—' she indicated the camera '—it's very kind of you.'

'*Prego.*' His gaze stopped at her bare feet, then

climbed back up. 'I wasn't sure what I'd hope for more on my return—to find you still in my bed or to have the temptation of making love to you again taken away from me by you being out of it. Not that a bed is necessarily a means to an end.' The grim delivery of his words made her heart drop further into despair.

'You don't sound like you would've preferred the former option.'

His ragged laugh as he veered towards the kitchen caught at her insides. 'Trust me, *cara,* I would've enjoyed it. I would take sweet oblivion with you over reality any day.'

She trailed behind him. 'So, you don't regret last night?'

The carton containing their breakfast landed on the countertop none too gently, followed by his phone. He came at her, stopping a bare inch shy of touching distance.

'I explored your body so thoroughly that every inch, every kissable freckle is imprinted on my memory. I should be sated but my hunger for you burns with a force that almost hurts. Right this minute I would love nothing more than to spread you over this counter, bury my mouth between your legs, lap my tongue over your sweet spot until you come for me, again and again. Does that sound like regret to you?' he breathed, his eyes fixed on hers in studied concentration.

Ava wasn't sure how it was possible to feel hot and cold at the same time. But she did. Somehow, she managed to croak, 'No.'

His body tight with tension, he stepped back and strode over to the coffee machine. 'I'll make another cup for you. This one's cold.'

'Cesare, what's wrong?' she asked because something was wrong. Desperately wrong. Despite her bold words, she quaked inside.

His shoulders stiffened, but he carried on pushing buttons. Only when the familiar sound of coffee percolating echoed through the kitchen did he face her.

'You know that bit in a movie when you know the good guy has done something really bad and is going to get it in the neck but you keep rooting for him anyway?'

Ava set her camera down before she dropped it. 'Yes?' Her voice emerged shaky.

'That's not me, Ava. I'm the bad guy, who selfishly took what he shouldn't have, then compounded his situation by making things a million times worse.'

'How have you made things worse?'

He shook his head as if words failed him. She

moved towards him, her feet hardly making a sound across the hardwood floor.

Cesare heaved a breath, struggled to calm the riotous feelings rampaging through him. He raked a hand through his hair, unable to bear the thought of telling her what he'd woken to—what the future held for them.

When he lowered his hand, Ava reached for it. He focused on her, his heart thumping now to a different beat, the hard pounding of want, of the selfish need to forget the last ten minutes. To go back and suspend time at the exact moment he'd woken up in Ava's arms.

But questions flooded her eyes—questions she'd grown so tired of asking but had never diminished nonetheless. What had she asked him? What was wrong? As if he'd spoken aloud, she nodded. 'Tell me,' she demanded firmly.

He tried to speak but the words wouldn't form. To speak would be to condemn him to hell for ever. But he'd known as he'd torn himself from Ava's warmth this morning and seen the missed call from Celine that he'd run out of time.

His hand tightened around hers and he led her to the living room and urged her down onto the sofa. He paced, yearning with everything inside him not to have to shatter her peace. She watched him, her expectant gaze gradually turning into a frown.

'For God's sake, whatever it is, just spit it out. Please,' she added, her plump lips trembling before she firmed them. 'You're scaring me with that bringer-of-the-Apocalypse look.'

Sucking in a breath, he sank down next to her. Immediately her evocative scent filled his nostrils. The urge to remain silent, to breathe it in and just drown in her heady essence almost overcame him. He suppressed a grimace.

He clasped his hands to stop their shaking. 'Celine called this morning but I missed it. I called her back ten minutes ago.'

The fear that entered her eyes chilled his heart. 'And?'

'She had the results. Roberto died from Late Onset Tay-Sachs syndrome.'

A shake of her head. 'I've never heard of it.'

'It's not a common condition. According to Celine, it is almost always misdiagnosed. Most people only know about it when it affects them.'

'Is it…did Roberto suffer?' she asked in a pained whisper.

His breath shuddered through his chest. '*Sì*. It's a horrible disease.'

When she put her hand on his cheek, he nearly

lost it. He greedily absorbed the touch because he knew it would be gone soon, once she knew the whole truth.

'I'm so sorry, Cesare. For you and for what Roberto went through.'

'Save your sympathy, *cara*. I don't deserve it.'

Her fingers trembled against his cheek. 'Why would you say that?'

'Because the condition…it doesn't begin and end with Roberto. It's a genetic defect that is passed down from parent to child.'

Her eyes remained blank, then slowly widened, filling with horror as the implications of his words finally sank in. Her hand dropped like a stone and she paled, the freckles dusted along her cheeks standing out against milk-white skin.

With everything inside, he wanted to take the pain away.

Ava fought to breathe. Moments ago, she'd been harbouring hope that they were about to discuss how to find their way back to each other.

Instead, he'd dropped this…this…

'Are you saying…that…you and Annabelle both have this gene?' The words scoured her throat.

Pain ripped across his face. 'Yes. I passed it to her. You called me bringer-of-the-Apocalypse. You were right.'

'But…she's perfectly healthy. Other than the odd cold, and what she suffered with the earthquake, she's never been sick a day in her life. And you're not sick either.'

'No, I'm…not.'

Something in his response caught her attention. 'Cesare, what aren't you telling me?'

His glance held a wealth of pain that made her heart lurch. 'Because both my parents carry the gene, what happened to Roberto could happen to me.'

'Did your parents know?'

'I'd like to think they wouldn't deliberately keep something like this from Roberto and me. I saw what losing him did to my mother. I'm guessing they don't know. Like I said, most people don't know they have it until they fall ill.'

For one blazing second she was fiercely glad his parents had been ignorant because they'd not only brought Cesare into her life, they'd also given her Annabelle. Then a thought trickled through, further chilling her blood.

'So what are the repercussions for Annabelle?'

His eyes took on a haunted look that stilled her heart. 'It could remain dormant all her life, or… the gene could mutate and she could develop complications,' he replied starkly.

A dark sound tore from her throat. Horror built, overcoming every other emotion as her insides screamed with disbelief at what he was telling her. Her daughter, her lovely daughter who had survived an earthquake, susceptible to a potentially life-threatening disease…

'Did you suspect something like this? Is that why you kept Roberto's illness from me?' The thought made her heart crack with pain. 'How long had he been seriously sick?'

'He'd been deteriorating for a year. It worsened in the last six months.'

Shock made her draw back, tears swiftly following as emotions tumbled through her. 'You knew all that, knew that something was very wrong and you kept it from me?'

He tried to reach for her. 'These were all second-hand reports. I didn't know just how bad he was. And I wanted to protect you—'

'Don't you dare say you were trying to protect me! You had no right to keep such a thing from me. What if Annabelle had fallen sick and I didn't know what was wrong?' Terror clutched her heart. 'Dear God, Cesare, what if she'd…' She couldn't voice the words. When he gripped her arms, she didn't move because she couldn't find the strength. Her insides felt numb and the horrific reality gripped her.

'Don't think like that.'

Slowly she raised her head. 'Why not? It's what you've been doing. At least now I understand the look you get when you look at Annabelle. You've been expecting the worst, haven't you?'

Cesare paled even more and the lines around his mouth compressed. 'I needed to be sure. It was why I postponed coming back to Bali. Roberto refused my attempts to see him. But six weeks ago, just before we left for Bali, he asked for me.' He sucked in a shuddering breath. 'He'd taken a turn for the worse. I think deep down he knew he wasn't going to make it. When I found out the extent of his illness, I contacted Celine. She tried to make him see a specialist but he refused. It was almost as if he'd given up…which was why we suspected suicide.'

'Oh God…' A strangled sob emerged.

His hands tightened on her arms. '*Cara,* I'm sorry—'

She wrenched away from him. 'You shouldn't have kept all this from me, Cesare.'

He gave a grim nod. 'I regret that. But I wanted to spare you the pain.'

'You had no right to shoulder this alone. We were

thousands of miles away. What if something had happened to you?' The thought brought a fresh bolt of horror.

'Nothing did. You had enough to deal with after the earthquake. I was not going to add to your distress.'

'That should've been *my* choice to make.'

Regret bit into his features. 'I told you, when it comes to you I seem to specialize in making bad situations worse.'

Her daughter—her precious baby girl—had a condition she'd never even known about. A deep shudder wracked her body. She tried to still her trembling but it got worse. A quick glance showed Cesare was caught in his own personal hell.

'Umm…the Apocalypse thing…I didn't mean it,' she muttered through stiff lips.

He gave a raw, pained laugh. 'But you were right.' He lifted a hand as if to touch her, then dropped it back down. 'Roberto shut himself off in Switzerland because of me. He suffered…alone for a long time because I didn't know how to reach him.'

Ava sucked in a breath. 'No. He shut himself off because he lost the love of his life, and decided to deal with it his way,' she said but Cesare wasn't listening.

'I keep thinking if I hadn't met Valentina in New York, hadn't given her a job, Roberto would've known some happiness…had the family he wanted.'

'Unless you have a direct dial to Fate, I think you can let go of that one. Some things you can control but sometimes things *just happen.*'

'The earthquake—'

'Just happened.'

'*Dio,* Ava, our daughter shouldn't have been there in the first place. You *saw* that marketplace in Bali. How could I *not* think she had been taken from us as payback for what I did to my brother?'

'You can choose to live in guilt for the rest of your life or you can choose to believe that ultimately you weren't responsible for Roberto. Even though you weren't close, you tried to look out for him. You took the woman he loved under your wing and tried to help, even when he blamed you for what happened in New York. I think you need to give yourself a break for that.'

He digested that for a while but, even though the pain in his face abated a little, his eyes remained haunted.

'As for Annabelle, she wasn't taken from us. We found her,' she added.

Another harsh laugh. 'Yeah, we did. And look

what I've delivered to her fragile life. You have to face the fact that I'm bad for you, I have been since the moment we met. But…' He shoved a hand through his hair.

'But…? You're going to walk away again?'

'No!' He lifted his gaze, and Ava's heart stopped at the gut-wrenching bleakness in his eyes. 'I can't. Annabelle is my flesh and blood, the most important thing in my life.'

Ava's gut tightened until she couldn't breathe. 'And since I've made us a package deal you're stuck with me too, right?'

'I didn't say that—' He surged up beside her as she stood. 'Where are you going?'

She shoved a hand through her hair, unable to stop the terror churning through her belly. 'I can't stay here—'

'You can't leave!' He grabbed her arms. 'We haven't finished talking.'

'Why? Is there another bombshell you're going to hit me with?'

'No, but we need to discuss what happens next and I—'

'I…need some air. I have to think.' His grip tightened. 'Let me go.'

'Ava, please. Stay.'

Her breath snagged in her lungs. 'Why?' Her

question was soft because of the tears clogging her throat and because she didn't dare to give life to the vain hope flaring inside. 'Why do you want me to stay?'

Silence greeted her question. Then, 'Because you are my wife. I made a vow to protect you and I believed I was doing the right thing by not burdening you with Roberto's news.'

Pain ignited inside her. She barely managed to remain standing, so strong was the grief that wracked her. 'You took other vows, too, Cesare. Or have you forgotten?' The words scraped her throat.

'They weren't as important as your protection.' An unfamiliar note altered his tone. Her heart hammered as she tried to read his expression. But his face remained inscrutable, his eyes a cool, impenetrable wall as he returned her stare.

'No. I suppose to you they weren't.' Unable to withstand his gaze, she turned away. He didn't stop her walking away.

All through her shower she felt numb. A part of her wanted to get into the first taxi, go and grab her daughter and hug her close. The other, more rational part of her knew she had to get her emotions under control before Annabelle returned. For her daughter's sake, she knew the latter decision was best.

Dressed in white linen trousers and an aqua silk-trimmed cotton top, she caught her hair up in a bun and slipped the camera strap over her head.

When she entered the living room, Cesare stood exactly where she'd left him, but the tiny espresso cup in his hand showed he'd busied himself with other things. His face was devoid of expression as he gulped it in one smooth swallow, set the cup down and came towards her.

Ava backed away. 'I…what time are your parents bringing Annabelle back?'

'After lunch, but we can make it sooner or later. Just say the word.'

She shook her head. 'After lunch is fine. I…I'll make sure I'm back by then.' She headed for the door, and stopped when he fell into step beside her.

'What are you doing?' she demanded.

'I'm coming with you.'

'No, you're not. I told you, I need some air.'

'There's enough air out there for both of us, I'm sure.'

'I meant alone.'

'Out of the question. You're reeling from the news I've laid at your feet. I recognize that, as the person who's caused you pain, I'm the last person you want around you, but you're my responsibility nonetheless.'

'What? Suddenly your *security detail* isn't up to the job?'

'Why delegate when I'm in the position to do a better job?'

'*Now* you choose to play the attentive husband?'

His jaw tightened. 'I married you. I brought this chaos to your doorstep. And I'm damned if I'm going to abandon you now to deal with it alone. We deal with it together. And call me selfish, Ava, but I'm hoping staying with you will earn me your forgiveness quicker. And, who knows, if I manage to save you from being hit on by a mercenary local, then I may even gain some Brownie points.'

Her hand tightened around the camera. Looking at him, at the visible distress in his face, made the tightness in her chest loosen a little. 'It's not going to be that easy, Cesare. To be honest, I don't even know what I'm feeling right now.'

He nodded. 'Then we won't talk. Just walk, *sì*?' He moved past her and held the door open.

With a sigh, she went through it and waited while he called up the lift.

They walked for an hour without speaking, heading west instead of east where most of the popular Roman landmarks were located. Ava concentrated on documenting the local life.

But, even lost in the one thing she loved to do

most aside from being a mother, she was hyper-aware of Cesare's pain-ravaged presence beside her. The part of her that acknowledged he must be reeling wanted to offer comfort. But her own shock was too great to process.

He might have suggested they wouldn't talk but she soon realised he had no intention of keeping his hands to himself—a hand in the small of her back to guide her across the street; around her waist to steer her clear of a group of excited tourists or a careless scooter, or a touch on her shoulder to draw her attention to a statue or a fresco he thought she might be interested in.

When the sun rose higher, he led her to a small local shop and bought her a wide straw hat, sun cream and a bottle of water.

Her breath caught as he squeezed a dollop of cream onto his fingers and applied it to her arms and face. When she lifted questioning eyes to his, his merely responded—*I don't want you to burn.*

Ava could've told him it was too late. She was already burning in hell. His every gesture demonstrated his regret for having kept Roberto's deterioration and death from her. Aside from that damning decision, everything else he'd done since had been to protect both her and Annabelle. Quietly, Ava had to concede that if she *had* been told so soon after nearly losing Annabelle in the earthquake, she wasn't sure she would've withstood the blow.

Her thoughts scattered when Cesare's arm slid around her shoulders. When she glanced at him, he nodded at a *trattoria* across the square overlooking the Tiber.

'We skipped breakfast. And also I think it's time to get out of the heat.'

Although she suspected she wouldn't be able to hold down a single mouthful, she reluctantly nodded.

The owner broke into a smile and ushered them in the moment he recognized Cesare. After they were seated in a far corner of the cool *trattoria,* Cesare ordered *cornetti,* fruit and coffee, along with a selection of sliced Parma ham.

Once they were alone, he sat back and watched her with narrowed eyes.

'I…haven't forgotten that in all this you've also received a horrible shock,' she said in a low voice. 'I'm sorry.'

'Does that mean I'm not in Hades any more?' he murmured.

She plucked the hat from her head and set it down on the spare chair along with her camera.

'First of all, I want to know everything about this condition, and I mean everything. No protecting me from the unsavoury facts.'

'I don't want you to worry about—'

'No, Cesare. I want to know *everything!*'

His lips firmed but he nodded. 'Celine emailed me a report. I'll forward it to you.'

'Also, we have to tell Annabelle—'

'No, she's too young to understand.'

After a second she nodded. 'Okay, but as soon as she's old enough, we'll tell her. I don't want her kept in the dark.'

'*Sì,* I agree.' He met her surprised gaze with a mocking smile. 'You see, I'm learning the error of my ways. Which brings me to another subject.'

'What subject?'

'Us,' he stated baldly.

'Did we not agree only a few nights ago that there was no *us*?'

'I think in light of recent developments, we need to revise that view.'

'Recent developments…you mean us having sex? That changes anything, how?'

His hands fisted until his knuckles turned white. 'Are you saying it doesn't?'

A dart of pain arrowed through her. 'You said it yourself, Cesare—the sex has always been mind-blowing between us, but it doesn't form the basis of a sound relationship, let alone marriage. I need more.'

His normally golden features paled. He opened his mouth but, before he could speak, their waiter approached, platters held high. Cesare's gaze remained fixed on hers the whole time the owner fluttered around them in effusive Italian. After a minute, he fell into silence when he realised neither of them paid attention.

The second he left, Cesare rasped, 'And if I'm unable to give you more?'

She shrugged. 'I'll do anything and everything to ensure Annabelle remains healthy and safe. Between us we can plan for one of us to always be with her. I'll make sure that works for any future assignments. But when it comes to you and I, Cesare, unless something changes drastically between us other than the mind-blowing sex, I don't see why we need to stay married. Do you?'

CHAPTER ELEVEN

THEIR SECOND ATTEMPT at breakfast failed. Miserably. Neither of them could summon the words to reassure the *trattoria* owner that it wasn't the food.

When Cesare grimly collected her things and marched her out into the sunlight, Ava was more than ready to leave. Paolo was parked on the kerb, a fact which didn't surprise her one little bit. Cesare was worth billions, after all, which meant he could probably summon his car with a mere thought.

He slid in beside her on the limo's back seat and sent up the partition.

'Ava...'

'Please, can we go and get Annabelle? I want to see my baby.'

His lips compressed for a second. Then he nodded. Pulling his phone from his pocket, he made a call, presumably to his parents. Minutes later he ended the call.

'They've taken her to the zoo. We can collect

her from there once we get our things from the apartment.'

'I don't want—'

'Don't worry, I won't force you to have this conversation now. But it will be discussed.'

'What is there to discuss? I won't subject myself to a marriage based on sex.'

'Last night's events suggested differently. Are you sure you're not refusing to consider us because of another reason?' A shadow of vulnerability echoed through his words.

It took a couple of seconds for her to grasp his meaning. 'You think just because we've discovered you carry a defective gene, I'm taking the opportunity to bail out of a marriage *you* didn't want in the first place? You're unbelievable, Cesare.'

He had the decency to redden. 'So you still maintain your need for a family above everything else?'

'Yes. I want a family, and that's not what you've offered. You've offered distance, secrets and the occasional sex marathon. I want to be needed; I want to be loved. I want you to come to me when you have a problem, not turn to your childhood friend or deal with it alone. God, you don't trust me, not even when it comes to sex.'

He frowned. 'What are you talking about?'

'Last night, in bed…you…you pulled out before

you… The first time I thought I'd imagined it. Then you did it again. I don't have to be a genius to work out that the last thing you want is to get me pregnant again!'

He cursed under his breath. 'Why does that surprise you? You got pregnant with Annabelle despite my use of condoms and you being on the Pill.'

'Can't you see what's wrong? Once again, *you've* decided, without asking me how I feel about it.'

'And if we'd had the talk you so desperately craved last night, if I'd laid all my cards on the table, would you still have come to my bed?'

'I guess we'll never know now, because you didn't.'

'*Santa cielo,* I can't believe you're condemning our marriage based on the fact that I won't come inside you!'

Heat engulfed her face and neck. 'You're vile! I'm condemning our marriage because you've never trusted me enough to tell me the things that matter!'

'I've told you everything!'

'How do I know? You didn't even tell me Roberto had died. I have to drag everything out of you. Well, guess what? That *machismo* thing may be sexy for a while, but it wears thin eventually, especially when you know I'm not a wallflower who's scared of my own shadow. Face it, Cesare. Even though you claim not to, you're still trying to protect me. And it hurts.'

Relief shot through her when she realised they'd reached the apartment. She lunged for the door and was halfway to the lift before Cesare caught up with her.

'Ava, stop—'

Her phone pinged and she pounced on it. Seeing the message, her fury grew. 'For the love of sweet baby meerkats, please tell Agata Marinello you're not going to her son's wedding *before I kill her!*'

In silence, he withdrew his phone from his pocket and tapped in a few keys. 'It is done.' The lift came and he stepped in after her.

Just before the lift shut, her phone pinged again. Her mouth dropped open at the effusive message displayed on her screen.

'*You're going to the wedding?*'

He eyed her with a mixture of triumph and determination.

'*Sì.* I've messed up big time where we're concerned. But I'm owning it now.'

Her heart hammered. 'What does that mean—you're owning it?'

'It means you're not going to get rid of me that easily, *mia bella moglie.*'

* * *

When they picked Annabelle up an hour later, Ava had to restrain herself from smothering her child in hugs while Cesare stood a distance away talking to his parents. Her heart tightened when she saw the stricken look on their faces.

As he hugged his mother and shook his father's hand, she contented herself with holding Annabelle's hand as she was regaled with tales from the giraffe pen and the varied animals she'd become best friends with at the zoo.

In the car, she fought back tears, especially when she caught Cesare's bleak stare.

'How are your parents?'

His haunted gaze connected with hers. 'They didn't know and they'll need time to process it. I've arranged for the specialist to speak to them and I plan to speak to them myself in a few days.'

She nodded and glanced at Annabelle, then blinked back more tears as emotion welled up.

'Mummy! You're not listening.'

'Yes, I am, sweetie. You're telling me how tall the giraffes were.'

'No, I *said* the leopard had *millions and millions* of spots.'

'Oh yes, of course, the leopard…' Her gaze caught Cesare's and her heart tripped at the sheen of tears in his eyes. Pushing aside her own pain, she grasped his hand and felt it tighten around hers.

Her life might have fallen down a rabbit hole, but her reason for living—her daughter—was also Cesare's reason for living. She had no doubt about that now.

They got to Lake Como by mid-afternoon. Although she protested long and hard, Annabelle eventually went down for a nap after a quick swim with Cesare.

Ava immersed herself in the last preparations for the wedding. She chose three of her best cameras, then, after a short contemplation, added the newest camera.

She reached for it and, almost on automatic, clicked onto the pictures of Cesare she'd taken that morning. Pain tightened in her chest as she read the meaning behind his anguish. Without warning, the tears she'd held at bay prickled her eyes. The faster she dashed the tears away, the quicker they fell.

'Ava?'

She stiffened. 'Not now, Cesare. I'm going to need a bit more time to deal with this.'

He came closer. Of course he did. 'You're crying.' His observation sounded hugely pained.

'I suppose you're going to order me to stop.'

'I learned a long time ago that I can't order you to do anything, *cara*. But I would like you to tell me why you're crying.'

'So you can add it to the list of things to protect me from?'

'So we can work through it.'

A bitter laugh scratched her throat. 'Do the words *too little too late* mean anything to you?'

He sat down next to her and every cell in her body reacted to his heat and proximity.

'We haven't reached there yet.' Without warning, he reached out and took the camera from her. Tense silence permeated the living room as he clicked through the pictures. When he'd finished, he turned off the camera and placed it on the large antique table where she'd been working. 'If those pictures moved you to tears, then we're not as irredeemable as you make out.'

Her lips firmed. 'Maybe they were cathartic tears, the *I'm-moving-on* type.'

He reached out and pulled her close, one hand capturing her nape to hold her steady. Tilting her chin with his thumb, he looked deep into her eyes. 'You're hurting for me, for us. And, as much as I would like to take your pain away, I'm learning that it's *your* pain; you have to deal with it. I don't like to see you cry, of course, but don't tell me to walk away when you're hurting.'

She tried to swallow past the huge lump lodged in her throat. 'Stop it, Cesare.'

'Stop what?'

'Stop teasing me with the promise of the man I thought I married. I can't take it.'

A grim smile curved his lips. 'We'll get through this, *cara*.'

Tears surged again. 'I really don't see how.'

'We agreed on a truce on your first day back. I know the past few days have rocked that a little.'

She gave another laugh. 'That's the understatement of the millennia.'

He leaned in and pressed his lips against hers. Heat surged through her, desire drenching her in a heady rush. When he pulled away, she nearly moaned in protest. 'It's strong enough to hold for a little while longer, at least until after the Marinello wedding on Saturday. We'll get away from here, go to the vineyard in Tuscany for a few days, yes?'

The promise of a reprieve, of not having to make a decision one way or the other about the state of her marriage, was one she welcomed, despite the full knowledge that it was only temporary. At Cesare's insistent look, she nodded. 'Yes.'

'*Bene*. I've told Lucia to serve dinner early. She's

making your favourite—*fettucine ai funghi.* I'm hoping this time we'll make it past the seeing-but-not-eating stage.'

On cue, her stomach growled. Cesare gave a low laugh and released her. 'You finish up here, I'll go and wake up Annabelle.'

'Okay…wait!'

He turned at the door.

'You were going to give me the information on Tay-Sachs.'

A wary gleam entered his eyes but he nodded. 'We'll look at it together after dinner.'

Her heart hammered as she watched him walk away, his powerful shoulders and tall, streamlined body reminding her just what she stood to lose if she decided to walk away from him.

Confusion crowded her senses, along with the undeniable knowledge that the reason why she was in so much pain was because she'd never really stopped loving Cesare. If anything, the rare glimpses into the man underneath all that control—the man who, despite his brother's rejection, had done everything he could for Roberto—made her love him even more.

Far from what he led her to believe, family meant a lot to Cesare. His brother had meant a lot to him despite their rocky relationship, and she'd seen him remain strong for his parents.

Which meant it was *her* he didn't feel the ultimate connection to.

Would that ever be enough without his love? *What of the alternative?* The thought of never being with Cesare intensified her pain until she couldn't sit still any longer.

Jumping up, she grabbed her oldest camera, a gift from her mother the year before she died. The camera Cesare had given her was worth thousands of euros, but this one was priceless. Every time she used it, she felt closer to the mother who'd believed and championed her desire to be a photographer when her father had scoffed at the idea.

Her mother had protected her against her father's bullying right up until the moment she'd lost her battle against cancer. Ava's devastation had been all the more acute, because with her mother gone, she'd lost not only a parent but an ally and protector. Her father had barely acknowledged her existence, and her brothers had soon followed suit.

For a long time, her camera had been her only companion...until Cesare.

Could she bring herself to let him go? Or would staying to fight, to push for what she wanted only drive him further away?

Shaking her head, she went out onto the terrace and walked down the jetty. The setting sun hung between the hills, its orange-gold rays a perfect backdrop for the yachts on the lake. The rich vibrancy of Lake Como in summer was a beauty to behold and, even though it didn't soothe her troubled soul, she took several pictures, her fingers clicking automatically.

Hearing voices behind her, she turned. Cesare stood on the edge of the terrace, Annabelle in his arms. Something she said made him laugh and Ava's heart caught at the love she glimpsed in his face. Acting quickly, she snapped a few shots of them. Cesare glanced up, straight into the camera, and the want, the need as his gaze connected with the lens stopped her breath.

She wanted to believe, yearned to trust what she saw in his face. But how could she, when her heart felt ripped to pieces?

'Be warned—our daughter has tasked us to bring back the perfect princess gown. Apparently it has to be purple. With pictures of giraffes on it.'

Ava summoned a smile as she buckled her seat belt. 'At least it's not pink.' She shuddered.

Cesare slammed the door and turned the ignition to the luxury SUV. '*Sì*, that *is* a small mercy.

However, I'm at a loss as to where to acquire such a dress.'

'Ah, welcome to the challenges of parenthood.'

He looked worried. 'Seriously, you didn't see the look on her face when she told me what she wanted. I don't think I'll survive if I don't bring her exactly what she wants.'

Despite the despair ravaging her soul, she laughed. 'We'll find something that will please her, I promise. But you didn't have to come shopping with me. I could've sorted this out on my own.'

So far the truce was going well. It had gone slightly wobbly when Cesare had presented her with the dossier containing information on the genetic condition two nights ago. Seeing the stark words in black and white had sent her into another crying jag, one which Cesare had withstood with silent, unwavering support.

Tay-Sachs was a horrible disease, and her heart bled for what Roberto had gone through; what Cesare *could* still go through. Annabelle was less likely to suffer the same fate as Ava wasn't a carrier but she would need monitoring all of her life, a fact that had struck fear anew in Ava's heart.

'What makes you think only women have the right to the *I don't have a thing to wear* line?' His query brought her back to the present.

'Yeah, right. You hate shopping with such a passion that you instruct top designers to send you their collection at the start of the season so you don't have to lift a finger. Which makes me think you're only coming along because…' She paused.

He shot her a heat-filled look. 'You would be right. I'll take any moment I can with you, even if I have to endure a few brain cells committing *hara-kiri* while you shop.'

He joined in when she laughed. 'That is *not* the way to make a girl feel special. But thank you.'

His right hand left the steering wheel, caught hers and brought it to his lips. Heat drenched her and although her heart surged with foolish delight, a part of her clenched in distress. This was the part of the truce that wasn't going so well. By mutually unspoken agreement, they hadn't discussed sex. Or the distinct lack of it. At night, they went to their separate beds, where Ava endured either tortured yearning-for-Cesare dreams or hours of wide-awake craving-Cesare tossing and turning.

Another kiss on the back of her hand recaptured her attention. His darkened eyes told her he was struggling with this part of their truce too.

Unable to dispel the atmosphere, she plucked her shades off the top of her head and slid them on. Not that it helped one iota. 'Let's go.'

She found her dress in an exclusive designer shop in Amalfi. And, despite thinking it impossible, they found the perfect purple gown for Annabelle.

'Those aren't giraffes, *cara,*' Cesare muttered, the worry back in his eyes.

'No, but she loves purple horses just as much. We just have to manage her expectations a little bit.'

His lips firmed as he handed over his platinum card. 'If she threatens to annihilate me with those adorable green eyes, I *will* use you as a human shield.'

'Wow, I never thought I'd see the day when you'd be slayed by a three-year-old.'

'She's almost *four.* And you haven't been watching, *tesorio mio.* I was slayed a long time ago.'

Every single breath whooshed out of her lungs as she stared into Cesare's golden eyes. He stared right back, a vulnerability lingering in his eyes she'd never seen before.

In that single moment, Ava knew she owed it to herself and Annabelle to find a way to make this work—even if it meant accepting less from Cesare.

The Marinello wedding took place in another stunning palazzo on the shores of Lake Como after the official blessing at the Duomo in Amalfi.

Cesare watched his wife, who, in a stunning

cream silk gown that bared her arms and back, and hugged her perfect backside, could've been mistaken for the bride, save for the camera slung around her neck. Despite that clunky accessory, she was a bombshell whose figure made his breath catch and his body burn with hunger every time he looked at her.

She was also scarily talented. Her work with the Marinello couple was displayed on a giant screen on the side of the ballroom where the reception was being held, and Cesare watched with pride as the guests effused over the stunning sepia and black and white pictures. Also, despite her threats to cause her bodily harm, Ava had managed Agata Marinello with a skill that left him awestruck. In the same circumstances, he wouldn't have been so kind to the shrill, demanding woman.

Lifting her camera now, she captured another image of the happy couple, then glanced down at the image. Raising her head, her gaze caught his. She tried to smile but he saw her distress. His insides churned.

They'd agreed to talk after the wedding but the back of Cesare's neck tingled with the premonition that time was running out. He had a toast to give—something Agata had sprung on him as they'd left the church—and several acquaintances and the Marinello family to acknowledge before he could reasonably get away.

He glanced Ava's way again. She was crouched, camera poised, as Annabelle and a newly made friend posed in front of her. This time her smile held a joy that made his own lips curve upward.

In the next moment, the alien feeling attacked him again. Sudden hunger clawed at his insides that had nothing to do with sex and everything to do with the unwavering feeling that he needed to act now or lose his wife.

Surging to his feet, he picked up a dainty sterling silver spoon and tapped it against his crystal champagne flute. His speech was a few minutes early but, what the hell. He had more important things to do. When he had everyone's attention, he racked his brain for appropriate words and made a reasonably coherent toast to the happy couple.

Duty done, he stepped from the VIP table and made a beeline for his wife.

'Your first dance is mine, I believe.' He caught her around the waist as the string quartet struck up.

'Cesare, I'm working!'

'I'm the guest of honour. If I choose to dance with the super-talented photographer of this wedding, then this is what I shall do.'

He drew her close, a deep satisfaction welling

up as she leaned into him. His body sprang to life, the unique scent of her making him ache.

Pulling her closer still, he teased his lips over her earlobe. 'I can't wait for this thing to be over.'

'It won't be for an hour or so yet. And then there's the evening reception—'

He frowned. 'That is unacceptable.'

She laughed. 'I was going to say I've got most of the pictures I need. Once the bride changes into her evening gown, I'll need a few more shots but, apart from that, I'm done. Agata wants to be the one to take the last picture of them leaving on their honeymoon. I didn't see the harm, so I don't have to stay till the end.'

He exhaled in relief. She heard it and pulled back to stare at him. His breath caught at how beautiful she looked.

'Why the urgency?'

'Other than the fact that you look breathtaking and I'm insanely jealous of any man who looks at you?'

One elegant brow arched. 'Try again.'

He sighed. 'I know we were going to wait until after the wedding to talk but…I've been going crazy not to be able to be with you. I've missed you in my bed.'

Her lips parted on a sigh and his blood rushed

forcefully south. She felt his body's reaction and stumbled. He used the excuse to bring her closer and watched her face bloom in a delicate blush.

'I…I thought we were putting everything on hold until Tuscany, including sex.'

'A foolish addendum. The moment we leave here I aim to resolve that.'

A look crossed her face that brought the feeling he'd experienced earlier back.

'And would sex come with strings?'

He frowned. 'What does that mean—*strings?*'

'I mean will you make love to me completely or will you…do what you did in Rome?'

Mild shock went through his body. 'Surely it can't mean that much to you?'

Her face flamed with the heat of a thousand candles, but she held his gaze. 'What if I said it did? What if I told you that when we were married—'

'We're *still* married.' He caught her left hand and, despite his displeasure at her bare fingers, he kissed the knuckle where her wedding ring should be.

She licked her lower lip and fire shot into his groin. 'I meant what if I told you that it's important to me because in that moment, when you lose control in my arms, I feel closest to you? That when you took that away from me I felt as if I've lost you completely? Would that change your mind then?'

Cesare froze. After several seconds, she pulled away. He couldn't find the strength to stop her.

'I thought not.' She left him on the dance floor, walking quickly away.

He didn't get a chance to talk to her again, not for another hour and not until Ava had taken her last picture and it was time to leave.

With Annabelle buzzing from making new friends and chatting incessantly, Cesare was forced to wait until they were back home. The chatter lessened as they drew closer to the villa and, by the time they were home, their daughter's head was lolling to the side.

'She's worn out,' Ava said.

'All day talking about horses and giraffes will do that to a girl. I'll put her to bed.'

'No, let me.'

'Ava...'

She avoided eye contact. 'I'll come and find you when I'm done with her.'

Cesare stood at the bottom of the staircase watching her walk away. The sinking sensation in his stomach intensified and for a wild second he wanted to rush after them, crush them in his arms and never let go.

Stemming the need, he turned towards his study. He needed to put the decision he'd made in the small hours of this morning into effect. It was the only way to ensure his family's safety. Once he was in possession of all the facts, he'd tell Ava. She would probably argue with him but at least they would talk it through together.

Ten minutes later, he was regretting not having left this phone call till morning.

'I've given you all the pertinent facts.'

He listened and blew out an exasperated breath. 'Yes, I've thought this through. Are you able to make it happen straight away or not?'

The stuttered protests echoing down the line sent a wave of irritation through him. Surging from his desk, he strode to the window, the phone clamped to his ear. 'No, I don't need my head shrunk. I *am* thinking straight. I know exactly what I want and I'm counting on you to make it happen… No, my decision is final…I definitely do not want any more children.'

The pained gasp that sounded behind him was the deadliest sound he'd ever heard. And even before he caught sight of Ava in the doorway, her face paler than he'd ever seen it, he knew he'd lost her.

CHAPTER TWELVE

UNCONTROLLABLE SHUDDERS RAKED through Ava. She couldn't catch her breath and the lack of oxygen made her head swim crazily. She squeezed her eyes, hoping to stem the relentless tide of hopelessness that threatened to drown her.

Even when she heard footsteps in the *salone,* where she'd retreated to, she couldn't move. For several minutes, Cesare stood behind her in silence, his breathing unsteady. Then firm hands settled on her shoulders. She flinched but when she tried to move away, he held on.

'Ava, listen to me.'

'No...' A weak, drained breath puffed out. His fingers tightened momentarily before he let go. She sensed him move away but she was too numb to lift her head.

Seconds later, he returned and held a glass against her lips. 'Drink this,' he commanded.

She caught a whiff of the cognac and jerked away from him. 'Getting drunk, as tempting as it sounds, isn't going to solve what's wrong with us, Cesare.'

'No, but it will help.' Contrition tinged his voice as he sat down beside her. 'It will also calm you long enough to let me explain.'

'What's there to explain? You spoke in English so I don't need anything interpreted—' She stopped as her phone buzzed. She was almost afraid to check the message; afraid that yet another blow would flatten her completely.

He caught her chin between his fingers and swung her to face him. Golden eyes narrowed immediately. 'You've been crying again,' he rasped.

'And this surprises you, why?' she shot back.

'We may drive each other completely insane at the best of times but I've only ever seen you cry once. Your natural reaction tends to be to claw my eyes out.'

'I must be getting soft in my old age.' Her phone let off another ping.

'Come on, Ava. You're clutching your phone. Has something happened? Something other than what you *think* you overheard just now? Tell me,' he demanded.

She tried to free herself. 'Why should I? You want me to share, and yet you don't reciprocate.' She jerked when her phone vibrated for the third time.

He glanced from her phone to her face. 'Who's calling you?'

A terrified breath whooshed out of her. Before she could stop them, her eyes filled with fresh tears. 'I feel as if my life's unravelling,' she murmured, more to herself than to him. From the moment she'd woken up in Rome, she'd felt as if the unstoppable avalanche of heartache she'd been running from was catching up with her—fast. 'Every time I think I have a handle on it, something else slips out of my grasp.'

'Nothing's slipped. *I* haven't slipped. I'm still here.'

'No, you're not. You like to think you're changing but you're still the same—'

'I'm here, Ava, and I'm not going anywhere. Tell me what's going on. Now.'

She shook her head and finally glanced down at her phone. 'The texts are from Nathan. He called me five minutes ago. My father's ill. He's asking for me.'

Cesare stared down at her bent head, the feeling he'd experienced on and off back in full force. Something wasn't right. It took a moment before he placed his finger on it. His feisty wife was sitting before him with her shoulders bowed, her beautiful skin paler than porcelain. Her fingers fretted with her phone.

The fire seemed to have gone out of her. And it scared the hell out of him.

Setting down the glass containing the amber liquor, he crouched before her. 'What did Nathan say? How bad is your father?'

Her lips tightened for a moment before she spoke. 'The doctors say it's his lungs…it started off as acute bronchitis but it's been complicated by pneumonia. His forty-a-day smoking habit hasn't helped. They don't know if he's going to make it.'

He slid his hands down her arms, thankful that she wasn't pushing him away. The thought that she didn't care enough to do so plagued him. 'Give me the full details and I'll get the best team of doctors to—'

'No. I won't be doing what *you* want, Cesare. Not this time.'

Alarm gripped the back of his neck. 'What do you mean? We're in this together. I'm only trying to help, *tesoro mio.*'

She finally lifted her gaze to his and the cool resignation in their depths stopped his heart. 'No, thanks. I've asked Nathan to find me a flight. There's a taxi coming to take me to the airport in fifteen minutes.'

Shock made him rock back on his heels but he quickly regrouped. 'Cancel the taxi. First of all, you're exhausted from running around at the wedding. We'll have an early night and take the jet tomorrow—'

She pulled away from him and jumped to her feet. 'You're still not listening to me, Cesare. I came downstairs to discuss what was happening between us, but also to say that I'm sorry for putting the burden of my wanting a family on you. It's what I've wanted for longer than I can remember but it wasn't fair to put it all at your feet. I want to be with you and Annabelle more than anything, so I hoped we could find some sort of compromise, but I can see now there's no hope for us, not if you're not willing to let me in even a little bit.'

The rise of hope and its subsequent swift death left him reeling. 'I...*sì*, we can—'

'Do you know why I've always yearned for a family?'

He nodded. 'Because you lost your mother when you were very young.'

'It wasn't just that. After she died, my father stopped seeing me—not that he'd paid me much attention to start with. But it was almost as if I'd ceased to exist in his eyes. When I dared to make myself heard, he would shut me down. Do you know how that feels? Being made to feel invisible? As if nothing I have to say or do matters?'

The icy stream that had drenched his veins solidified. 'Ava, please listen—'

'No, I'm done with controlling men.'

Her fire was back, and for that he was thankful. But he felt the distance between them widening with every second. 'I wasn't trying to control you—'

'Of course you were! *You* decided that Annabelle and I were better off without you, so you withdrew from us. *You* decided that I wasn't strong enough or was too upset to be told that Roberto was sick, and when he died you kept that to yourself, too. And…just now…' She sucked in a deep breath as her voice broke.

Desperate, he reached for her but she pulled away. He shoved his hands into his pockets. 'You didn't hear the full story just now. Let me explain.'

'I'm exhausted, Cesare. My father isn't an easy man to deal with at the best of times, and I seriously doubt he's had a sudden personality transplant, which means my visit is going to be a difficult one. I'd rather not use what little strength I have arguing with you.'

He pushed his fingers through his hair, anxiety and a previously unplumbed depth of fear coursing through him. If he let her walk out of here, would he ever see her again?

She's leaving Annabelle in your care. That counts for something.

With everything in him screaming to do otherwise, Cesare stepped back. 'Cancel the taxi, *cara*. Rest for a few hours before you make the trip. Paolo will drive you and the jet will be at your disposal. I'm sorry, but I'll have to insist on that. I won't let you travel while you're exhausted.'

His heart sank even lower when she merely shrugged and looked away.

He prowled the hallway, his eyes darting to the stairs, even though Ava had long gone to bed. He gave a short bark of laughter at the irony. Had it been only two weeks ago that he'd tried to stop her from returning? And now he wanted to do the reverse because everything inside him rebelled against letting her go.

He stopped in his tracks, stunned all over again by the feelings coursing through him. He could storm upstairs, articulate them to her, but he risked her thinking it was another controlling ploy.

He had to let her go and hope he would get her back. Barring that…

Clamping down on the roiling emotions tearing

through him, he strode into the living room. The discarded glass containing the cognac stood on the coffee table.

Picking it up, he knocked it back and sank onto the sofa. Fire and fear coursed a jagged path through his chest. The bottom of the glass mocked him.

Hell, he deserved more than mockery. To think that when he finally recognized his feelings, knew just what the woman he'd married meant to him, he couldn't tell her because he was too damned scared of losing her...

He tossed the glass onto the wooden table, saw it crack in two and barely gave a damn. Resting his head against the chair, he gritted his teeth against the need to do *something*.

It took the better part of an hour to accept that he could do nothing. Nothing but wait until Ava was ready to listen.

Cesare jerked awake and surged to his feet. The room was in semi-darkness. At some point some-one—most likely Lucia—had drawn the curtains and left a couple of table lamps burning. Without consulting his watch, he knew it was very late.

Probably too late...

He wasn't sure exactly what had woken him but

a feeling in the pit of his stomach sent him rushing from the room.

How arrogant of him to believe he could secure Ava's forgiveness just by telling her he'd been trying to protect her. *Dio,* how stupid was he?

He'd wounded his wife badly; he knew that now. But the thought of her walking away from him made him want to grab her and hold on as tight as ever.

He took the stairs three at a time. When his knock went unanswered, he pushed open her bedroom door. Her suite was empty. Fear clutching his soul, he rushed down the stairs, bellowing Lucia's name. He nearly collided with her as she emerged from the kitchen with one of the other maids in tow.

'Where is she?' he demanded.

The look she shot him was a cross between worry and disapproval. 'Signora di Goia? The taxi came for her an hour ago.'

A rush of blackness momentarily blinded him. 'What exactly did she say?'

The young maid answered. 'Nothing. She went to check on the *piccolina,* then come downstairs with her bag.'

He told himself to calm down, to think rationally. His inner voice just mocked him.

Returning to his study, he threw himself into his chair and clutched his head.

Cesare tried a mere half minute to talk himself out of it before he reached for his phone. His call went straight to voicemail. One minute later he tried again. After half a dozen tries, he left his first message.

Two hours later, doing everything to stem his terror, Cesare tried again. When Ava's husky tone instructed him to leave a message, he said the only thing he could think of.

An eternity later he ended the call and curled himself into the sofa, clutching his phone. Over and over, he told himself weeping was for the weak.

The good thing about travelling with one small bag was that she managed to clear Customs within minutes. The bad thing was that the temperature in London, even in early August, was rainy and damp enough to warrant a sweater. Shivering, she contemplated stopping to get one but quickly discarded the idea and headed for the exit.

Her hired car was ready and waiting. Twenty minutes later, she was driving down the familiar route towards the home she'd grown up in.

It was late, long past midnight, when she drew

up in front of the semi-detached house on the out-skirts of Southampton. The light in the upstairs window in what had been Nathan's room reas-sured her somewhat.

Quaking inside, she walked up the short path-way and pressed the bell.

Silence echoed after the jangling of the bell faded away, and then she heard feet thudding on the stairs.

Nathan's eyes lit on her. 'Ava, you came.' He stepped forward and enveloped her in a bear hug.

Surprised by the gesture, she drew in a shaky breath. 'Did you think I wouldn't?'

'I wasn't sure. You just said you'd think about it and then ignored my calls.'

'Is he awake? I need to speak to him.' Before she lost what little courage she had.

Nathan's eyebrows shot up and he checked his watch. 'Now?'

'Please, Nathan, it's important.'

He frowned, his brown eyes studying her face. 'What's happened, Ava?'

I think my marriage may be over and I want to know if I have any family left at all.

A hacking cough came from above and continued for a full minute. When it ended, Ava heard pain-ful heaving as her father tried to catch his breath.

Nathan's expression was pained. 'He's been having a hard time of it. It's worst at night—' He stopped when the phone rang.

Curious as to who would be calling so late, she stared questioningly at Nathan.

'It's your husband. He's been calling every ten minutes for the last two hours. Should I?' He indicated the phone.

She nodded, waited for Nathan to answer, then held out her hand. 'Hello, Cesare.'

'Ava, are you all right?' His voice was strained but the solid sound of his voice soothed a wounded, devastated place in her heart.

'Yes.'

'*Dio grazie.*' The mingled relief and pain in his voice made her heart clench. 'I'm glad you're safe but if you disappear on me like this again, I swear I won't be responsible for my actions,' he tagged on in a fierce undertone.

'I needed to do this, Cesare.'

'Just...' He stopped and inhaled audibly. 'I understand why you need to do this. I was the same with Roberto, even though he pushed me away. I told myself it didn't matter but every time...it hurt.'

'But you never gave up. You never stopped fighting for your family.'

The small silence made her heart stutter.

'No, I didn't. And I never will. I'll never stop fighting for us, Ava.'

This time her heart stilled. 'What are you saying?'

'Have you seen your father?'

'No, not yet. I just got here.'

'Before you do, I want you to know that, no matter what happens, I'll be here. Annabelle and I, we will be your family from now on. You never have to feel invisible or unwanted. And you don't have to settle for less than you want.'

Her grip tightened on the handset. 'Are you…do you know what you're saying, Cesare, because if this is just about protecting me—'

'Protecting you from pain and rejection will always be non-negotiable and, yes, I know I've caused a lot of it. But this is also about a lot more, *tesoro.*' He breathed a sigh of impatience. 'I don't want to do this over the phone, Ava. I want to see you. Are you coming back?'

'Do you want me to come back, Cesare?'

A disbelieving huff echoed down the phone. '*Sì,* of course I do! You are my wife, the mother of my child. I would be with you right now if you hadn't asked to do this alone. See? I'm learning.'

Her heart tripped at the fervent possessiveness and need in his voice. Foolish hope bloomed in her chest. 'You have to do a whole lot more if we're to get through this, Cesare.'

'I know. But…but don't give up on us…*per favore…*'

Her heart tightened along with her grip on the phone. 'I…I…'

'Don't say anything just yet. Did you listen to my messages?' She heard the touch of vulnerability in his voice and wondered at it.

'No, not yet.' She hadn't had time to turn her mobile back on.

'Okay. I've sent the jet for you. It will be at your disposal when you're ready to return but it would help if the pilot knew when that would be so he can file a flight plan.'

She smiled at the tactic, but the smile slowly faded when the enormity of what she had to do settled on her shoulders. 'Give me a day with my father.'

'Of course. I'll call tomorrow.'

She didn't miss the implacable nature of that promise. Hanging up, she turned to find Nathan hovering in the kitchen doorway.

'I'm going up,' she said.

He nodded.

Ava entered her father's room and found him propped up against pillows, his face coated in sweat despite the coolness of the night. His eyes were shut, but she knew he was awake because he clutched an oxygen mask over his nose and mouth.

'Hello, Dad.'

His eyes slowly opened. For a moment, a light, reminiscent of the stern figure he'd been, blazed in his eyes. Then slowly it faded. He pulled the mask from his face.

'Caroline...' he said weakly.

One hand attempted to lift off the bed, but feebly fell back down. Going to him, Ava took his hand, tears clogging her throat as she saw how withered, how frail he'd become.

The ogre who'd terrorised her childhood was now nothing more than a shadow of his former self. A shadow who'd mistaken Ava for his dead wife.

His watery eyes dimmed then another round of coughing interrupted whatever he'd been about to say. When it was over, he could do nothing more than inhale the oxygen and try to get his breath back.

'Don't try to speak, Dad. It's all right.'

Tears clouded her eyes and the pain she'd carried with her for so long slowly disappeared.

What her father had done in the past didn't matter any more. Hope flared in her heart. She and

Cesare had a lot to work through but Ava had hope—a hope that grew stronger with each passing moment.

Leaning down, she kissed her father's leathery cheek. 'I love you, Dad. I'm here for you. Sleep now.'

A laboured sigh escaped him and his eyes shut.

As she went downstairs and entered the kitchen, she activated her phone and saw twenty-six missed calls from Cesare. Before she could replay any of them, Nathan appeared with a cup of tea.

'Is everything all right?'

She nodded. 'Dad's sleeping.'

'I meant with you and your husband.'

Surprised, she looked up and caught Nathan's uncomfortable look. 'I know we weren't here for you when you were young. I guess that's why you didn't invite any of us to your wedding...'

'I didn't think any of you would come.'

He nodded. 'For what it's worth, I've missed you. I think Cameron and Matthew have too.' He looked away, shamefaced. 'Growing up, it was just easier to take Dad's lead, you know? It's no excuse, I know, but...heck, Ava, I'm sorry.'

Setting her cup down, she placed her hand over his. 'It's okay, Nathan.' At his sceptical look, she pressed on. 'It really is. I've made my peace with the past, and with Dad. At some point in the future, I'll try and reconnect with Cameron and Matthew too. I'd like Annabelle to meet her grandfather and uncles eventually.'

Nathan nodded, rose and touched her shoulder on his way out. 'I'm glad you're here,' he said gruffly. 'Goodnight.'

With tears clogging her throat, Ava abandoned her tea and went upstairs. After undressing, she slipped into her childhood bed. She felt comfort at being surrounded by the things she'd grown up with. Acting on a faint memory, she pulled open her bedside drawer. There it was, an old picture of her mother she'd kept even though her father had got rid of every last trace of her after her death.

Caroline Hunter had the same red hair as Ava and, despite her frail appearance, there was strength in her eyes that resonated within Ava.

She hadn't been able to beat cancer but, while she'd been alive, her mother had fiercely protected her daughter. Ava knew deep in her heart her mother would've done *anything* for her, protected her from any harm.

In his own high-handed way, wasn't that what Cesare had been trying to do? She might not agree with the way he chose to do it, but could she really condemn him for it? If their roles were reversed, what would she have done?

Ava gasped in the darkness as clarity shone beacon-bright. Pulling back the covers, she rushed out of her room and hammered on her brother's door.

'Nathan, do you have a computer I can use?'

'Now?'

She spent the rest of the night researching and by morning her decision was made.

Taking a deep breath, she took her phone out of her bag. Ignoring the countless messages that beeped at her, she searched until she found the right number.

It was answered on the third ring. *'Ciao?'*

'Celine, it's Ava. I'm sorry to disturb you so early.'

'Don't worry, life's too short for sleep anyway, right?' Her voice was light but Ava sensed the question behind her flippancy.

She cleared her throat and glanced out of the window overlooking the small, overgrown garden. 'I need your help.'

'Sure, anything you want,' Celine said.

With another deep breath, she outlined what she wanted.

'Ava, this is a huge step. Have you talked to Cesare about this?'

Guilt momentarily assailed her. She bit her lip and forged on. 'I need to do this. For us.'

'But…'

'Celine, please. Just help me.'

The other woman sighed. 'If your mind is made up—'

Ava rang off after she'd scribbled down the phone numbers of two reputable Harley Street practices. She rang the first one at nine. The doctor she requested was on holiday. She rang the second number, shamelessly name-dropped and was immediately put through.

After she explained what she wanted, the doctor made an appointment to see her the next day.

She spent the rest of the day with her father. He looked much better and even recognized her this time. In halting words often interrupted by acute coughing fits, he tried to explain why he'd treated her so badly.

Her mother had fallen sick almost immediately after Ava had been born. Irrational as he knew it to be, her father had secretly blamed her for losing his wife.

'It's not an excuse, but every time I saw you I was reminded of Caroline.'

Tears clogged Ava's throat. 'I'm sorry.'

'Don't apologise. What I did was wrong. I

pushed you away. I have no right to be, but I'm glad you're here.'

She left in a less sad mood than she'd arrived in.

Cesare might not love her but he cared about her enough to want her to return. Her heart tightened in pain at the thought that he might never love her as much as she loved him but whatever he felt for her…it was enough.

The drive to London took just over two hours and, all through the consultation, Ava told herself she was doing the right thing.

When the doctor finished talking through the procedure, she took a deep breath and signed the papers.

'How long will it be before I can go home?'

'If everything goes according to plan, you should be able to leave us in the morning.'

She could be back in Italy by nightfall tomorrow. The thought of seeing Cesare and Annabelle again sent a soft sigh of happiness through her.

Her phone pinged and she realised she'd never got round to listening to Cesare's messages the night before.

She scrolled through and pressed the first one.

When the nurse appeared to prep her for her procedure, she was stunned by the look on her patient's face.

* * *

Cesare cursed the traffic leading up into Regent Street, and resisted the urge to lean on his horn. Instead he made do with a string of coarse expletives as his heart lurched at what lay ahead of him.

What had she done? *Santa Maria,* what had his Ava done?

He'd already been on his way to the airport when Celine had rung in a panic. When he'd learnt exactly what his fiery, reckless, exceedingly breathtaking wife was planning, Cesare's blood ran cold.

Even as he sat here, uselessly inching his way forward in the godforsaken traffic, he could barely fathom it.

He gave into the urge and leaned on the horn. Rude gestures greeted his action, but he kept his hand in place until the driver in front crept forward enough for him to squeeze through.

Ten excruciatingly long minutes later, he slammed on the brakes and sprinted into the reception of the Harley Street practice.

When he announced himself, the receptionist's eyes widened.

'What room is my wife in?' he barked.

With a shaky finger, she pointed down the hall.

Cesare had never known such fear in his life as he skidded towards the door.

Dio, please let him not be too late.

Inside, Ava sat on the bed, her lovely hair tucked under a gruesomely ugly surgical hat. Her face was pale, but she wore the widest smile he'd ever seen as she pressed the button on her phone.

She hadn't seen him yet, her focus firmly on the phone. Cesare's breath caught as his voice echoed around the sterile room.

Ava, I know I've wronged you in the most hurtful way. But I am only mortal, cara, and this mortal loves you more than the fates will ever give me time on this earth to express. I promise to spend the rest of my life making amends, to giving you the family you've never had, if you let me. I will also let you go if that is what you ask of me. But please let me know you are safe, amore mio. I beg you.

'I can say it again in person, if you prefer.'

Her head jerked towards him, her stunningly gorgeous green eyes locking on his. Her smile slammed into his heart and he stopped breathing.

'*Cesare,* what are you doing here?'

Dio, he loved this woman. Loved her with a power that made his world tilt on its axis every time he looked at her.

'What am I doing here? Shouldn't *I* be asking you that? *What the hell are you thinking, doing this to me?*'

Despite her smile, her eyes rolled. 'I knew it was only a matter of time before it all became about you.'

She held out a hand to him. He swallowed and sent a silent prayer of thanks.

On seriously shaky legs, he approached the bed and took her hand. Warmth flowed from her. With another sigh of relief, he raised her hand to his mouth.

'Tell me you haven't gone through with the procedure—?'

'Not yet—'

'Not ever!' Several emotions coursed through him. He tried to keep it under control but they continued to shake right through him. 'Ava, why in God's name would you do this?'

'For the same reason you've been trying to find a way for us to be together. Last week in Rome before Celine called, what were you really going to talk to me about?'

'I was going to tell you there would be no divorce. I had no immediate solution but I was willing to do whatever it took to keep you and Annabelle in my life.'

'So you were ready to find a way to give me what I wanted.' He nodded. 'Well, I'm ready to do what it takes too. This is an equal opportunities marriage.'

'Yes, but this isn't your problem, *cara*. The Tays-Sachs aside, I let what happened with Roberto and Valentina shame me into suppressing what I wanted until it was almost too late. You and Annabelle are the most precious things in my life and I nearly lost you both.' He stopped, his breath shuddering out. 'I've accepted that I didn't handle things with Roberto very well and that I couldn't help him when he was in pain. It's something I have to live with.'

'Wherever he is, I'm sure he's at peace now,' she said.

He nodded. 'And I'll make peace with it some day. But not at the cost of my family. And not at the cost of this condition. I cannot...I won't let you take the burden on your shoulders.'

Although her heart lifted, a hint of shame stung her. 'I'm not without fault myself. What you said, about me putting you front and centre of everything I wanted in a family...you were right. After my mother died, dreaming of a perfect family was what kept me together. I was like one of those women you see sitting alone in a coffee shop, watching couples go past and doodling her imaginary husband and children's names on a napkin, only I used my camera. Then you appeared and I didn't stop to think of what *you* wanted…my whole focus was on making my dream come true. When you didn't immediately fall in line with my plans, I began to despise you for it.' She looked deep into his eyes, her heart laid bare. 'I'm sorry.'

With a deep groan, he pulled her tighter, kissed her until they were both out of breath. 'I'll forgive you if you give me a lifetime to make amends to you and to Annabelle for all the time I've lost with you.'

Her heart began to race. 'A lifetime?'

'*Sì,* non-negotiable.' He looked around the sterile room. 'And, speaking of non-negotiable, you accept that this is out of the question, don't you?'

'No. You've sacrificed enough for this family—'

'By walking away? By leaving you to care for our child on your own? How is that caring?'

'I was so hung up on finding a perfect family that I refused to see you were battling serious demons. I wanted you to be perfect for me and I had no right to do that. And the conversation I overheard on the phone, that was you arranging to have a medical procedure, wasn't it? You were willing to deny yourself a chance to become a father again just so you could hang onto us. What's that if not sacrifice?'

He clutched her hand tighter. 'I was going to discuss it with you first. I wasn't ready to give you up. Despite what I said in that message, I'm not and I never will be. But I don't want to risk passing this gene on to another child.'

She leaned forward and kissed him, and Cesare felt his heart stutter crazily.

'So let me do this. For us. It's time for me to lighten your load.'

'Absolutely not. You're not getting your tubes tied and I don't even want to hear the word hysterectomy.'

'Cesare—'

'It's out of the question!'

'You know, I'm sure there's a rule that says you can't yell at the patient.'

He didn't know whether to kiss her or shake the living daylights out of her. He contented himself with pulling the ugly cap off her head and stroking his fingers through her gorgeous fiery hair. 'Then you need to be nice to me.'

She frowned. 'What do you mean—be nice to you?'

'When Celine called and told me what you were planning, I called the doctor and altered the arrangement a little bit. No, don't death-stare me. We will discuss this first like a normal married couple. And then we will agree to do things my way.'

'You're having a vasectomy.' She didn't frame it in a question because she saw the resolution in his eyes.

'*Mio bella moglie,* this is something I have thought long and hard about.'

'I'll think about it, too, if you repeat the message you left on my phone.'

'Which one?'

'The one that says how you feel about me.'

'They all say how I feel about you. Each and every one of them ends with me telling you how much I love you.'

Her mouth dropped open. Unable to resist, he kissed her.

'Oh God, please say that again,' she whispered against his lips when they parted.

Her helpless plea stopped his heart. In fact, Cesare was sure he hadn't taken a complete breath since he'd walked into the room. The enormity of the sacrifice she'd almost made swept him away.

Tears prickled his eyes and he squeezed his jaw tight to stem the flow. But he knew he'd failed when he felt wetness on their entwined fingers.

'I love you, Ava *mia.* I'll spend the rest of my life proving how much I love you.'

'I love you too, so much my heart bursts with it.'

Ava felt her heart lift at the complete adoration in her husband's eyes. Tears fell freely from her eyes as she basked in Cesare's love. When he leaned over and brushed them away more fell.

Gently, he cupped her face and smoothed his thumbs over her cheeks. Then, leaning forward, he kissed her eyes closed. '*Amore,* don't cry. I hate seeing you cry.'

'Get used to it. I intend to cry very often.'

'But only tears of happiness, *sì?*' he asked desperately.

'Maybe. I can't promise that any more than I can promise not to turn into a scream-with-happiness girl.'

'Whichever you decide to be, I'll be by your side, loving you.'

Ava's heart leapt and basically did crazy things that would've scared the doctors had they known about it. Cesare kissed her again and kept on kissing her until the nurse found the courage to knock on the door. The almost indecent scene she found made her hesitate before giving a delicate cough.

'The doctor's ready for you now, Mr di Goia. If you'd like to come with me, please?'

Ava grabbed him when he started to move away. 'Sorry, change of plan. We're both leaving.'

Cesare frowned. 'Ava?'

'If I'm not having the procedure, neither are you. We'll find another way. Together. Yes?'

His eyes shone with love as he nodded. 'Together.'

EPILOGUE

'ARE YOU ALL right?' Cesare whispered in her ear as they watched the old, gaily painted SUV travel slowly up the driveway.

'No,' Ava whispered back.

A deep masculine laugh caressed her lobe. 'Why can't you be like other women and say, *Yes, I'm fine, thanks*?'

She grinned and faced him. 'Where's the fun in that?'

'For a start, it would cause me less heartache.' He caught her fingers in his hand and kissed the di Goia wedding emerald he'd placed back on her finger the day he'd come for her in London.

She placed her hand over his heart and delighted in his hitched breath as it skipped a beat. 'I see what you mean.' When she went to remove it, he placed his hand over hers. He looked over her head at the advancing car.

'Do you think they'll like us?' His voice was tinged with anxiety.

Ava marvelled at the change in the strong, self-possessed man she'd renewed vows with six months ago. Cesare hadn't lost any of his endless self-assurance, but he'd become more open, more in touch with his feelings in a way that made her love him even more than she'd ever dreamed possible.

They'd agreed to go ahead with Cesare's vasectomy—he'd been too tortured by the idea of passing on his Tay-Sachs gene to any future children—but only after Ava had insisted on gene therapy and a rather large sperm bank deposit. The idea of a vasectomy reversal had also remained firmly on the table.

So, whatever the future held, they had options.

For now, though, one decision they'd made together had come to fruition.

She leaned up and planted a swift adoring kiss on his lips. 'Cesare, the babies are six months old. The likelihood that they'll fall in love with you at first sight is very, very strong. Trust me.'

The vehicle stopped and two women alighted. Cesare, with his arm still around her, stepped forward to greet them. The moment he smiled, they melted.

Dear heaven, even nuns weren't immune to her husband's charm.

Smiling too, she descended the stairs and greeted the two nuns who ran the orphanage in Amalfi. After introductions were made, Ava led them into the *salone* before, heart thumping wildly, she brought herself to glance into the twin car seats.

There, lying sweetly beneath their blankets, were their son and daughter. Their approval for adoption had gone through two weeks ago. Her heart skipped in joy as *Suor* Rosa pushed the first seat gently towards her.

'Here is Maria. Her afternoon naps are very precious to her, so be warned.'

Suor Chiara smiled and handed the second seat to Cesare. 'And this is Antonio.'

Cesare glanced into the car seat and his eyes misted. She knew he was remembering Roberto.

'He's the quieter of the two, but he has a very strong will,' *Suor* Chiara said.

Cesare gazed down silently at his son, then lifted a hand to brush the baby's cheek. 'He will grow into a handsome man, just like his uncle.'

'No. Just like his father,' Ava murmured to him.

He smiled at her, a smile so filled with love her heart turned over.

An hour later, the nuns left. Ava stared at Cesare and he returned her look with an equally bewildered expression. 'Three children. Are we mad?' he asked.

'Quite possibly,' she said, laughing. 'So, shall we show them to their room?'

Inhaling audibly, he nodded. They picked up the seats and were barely in the hallway when an exclamation of delight sounded behind them. They turned as Annabelle flew towards them. 'The babies are here!'

Cesare stopped and introduced his daughter to her siblings.

Annabelle lifted wide eyes to her. 'Mummy, can I go show them my room? I'll share my toys with them, I promise. So can I? Can I?'

'That's a brilliant idea, sweetheart. I'm sure they'll love that.'

Annabelle whooped. Over the top of her head, Cesare's eyes met hers. His smile blew her clean away.

'I love you,' he murmured.

'Right back at you, *caro*,' she echoed.

* * * * *

Mills & Boon® Large Print
February 2014

THE GREEK'S MARRIAGE BARGAIN
Sharon Kendrick

AN ENTICING DEBT TO PAY
Annie West

THE PLAYBOY OF PUERTO BANÚS
Carol Marinelli

MARRIAGE MADE OF SECRETS
Maya Blake

NEVER UNDERESTIMATE A CAFFARELLI
Melanie Milburne

THE DIVORCE PARTY
Jennifer Hayward

A HINT OF SCANDAL
Tara Pammi

SINGLE DAD'S CHRISTMAS MIRACLE
Susan Meier

SNOWBOUND WITH THE SOLDIER
Jennifer Faye

THE REDEMPTION OF RICO D'ANGELO
Michelle Douglas

BLAME IT ON THE CHAMPAGNE
Nina Harrington

0114 Rom LP

Mills & Boon® Large Print

March 2014

MILLION DOLLAR CHRISTMAS PROPOSAL
Lucy Monroe

A DANGEROUS SOLACE
Lucy Ellis

THE CONSEQUENCES OF THAT NIGHT
Jennie Lucas

SECRETS OF A POWERFUL MAN
Chantelle Shaw

NEVER GAMBLE WITH A CAFFARELLI
Melanie Milburne

VISCONTI'S FORGOTTEN HEIR
Elizabeth Power

A TOUCH OF TEMPTATION
Tara Pammi

A LITTLE BIT OF HOLIDAY MAGIC
Melissa McClone

A CADENCE CREEK CHRISTMAS
Donna Alward

HIS UNTIL MIDNIGHT
Nikki Logan

THE ONE SHE WAS WARNED ABOUT
Shoma Narayanan

0214 Rom LP